THE

GREAT

WALL

OF

LUCY

WU

THE GREAT WALL OF LUCY WU

WENDY WAN-LONG SHANG

SCHOLASTIC INC.

This book was originally published in hardcover by Scholastic Press in 2011.

ISBN 978-0-545-16216-6

12 11 10 9 8 7 6 5 4 3 2 1   13 14 15 16 17 18/0

Printed in the U.S.A. 40
This edition first printing, January 2013

The text type was set in Adobe Garamond Pro Regular.
The display type was set in Infinite Bold and Folio Bold Condensed.
Book design by Marijka Kostiw

FOR

MY MOTHER

AND

HUSBAND

PROLOGUE

<small>THERE IS A CHINESE STORY THAT GOES LIKE THIS:</small>

An old man lived at the edge of the northern frontier. One day, his horse ran away, and the neighbors came to comfort him. What a loss! But the old man didn't worry. "This may turn out to be good," he said.

Sure enough, a few days later, his horse returned, bringing another horse with it. This new horse was beautiful and swift. Now the neighbors complimented the old man on his good fortune. "While it is true that I have gotten this other horse for free, something bad may happen," replied the old man.

The old man had a son who loved this new horse, and he often took it out to race in the fields. One day, the son fell off the horse and broke his leg. The neighbors shook their heads at the man's bad fortune, but the old man was not concerned.

Shortly after that, the emperor called up all the young men in the kingdom to fight in a war. The son of the old man could not go because of his broken leg, but many other young men lost their lives in the bloody battles that followed.

In Chinese, if you want to say that something good may turn into something bad, or vice versa, you say, *Sai weng shi ma*, or *The old man at the frontier lost his horse.*

I wish I had known this saying when I thought I was going to have the perfect year.

CHAPTER ONE

When I think back on it, I'd have to say that it all started with the Golden Lotus. The Golden Lotus is a famous Chinese restaurant, about two hours away from where I live. It is a long way to go for dinner, as Mom pointed out to Dad when his cousin first invited us to come for a birthday party.

Dad said, "I haven't seen B.D. for years and my uncle is turning seventy-five—we should go."

My big sister, Regina, squealed, "The Golden Lotus is supposed to be amazing! We *have* to go. They have Peking honey bananas."

My big brother, Kenny, said, "I'm in. Chinese banquets are seriously loaded."

I said, "Mamma Lucia's is having a pizza and pasta special on Saturday and they're showing the NBA All-Star Game on the big screen." Guess who didn't get her way?

When we walked into the Golden Lotus, though, even I had to admit that it was the most beautiful restaurant I had ever been to. The first thing I saw were dozens of glittering, sparkling chandeliers hanging from the ceiling. The carpet was thick and springy, with an intricate pattern of medallions and flowers on a royal blue background. The hostess was really pretty, too, dressed in a red *qipao* and matching high-heeled sandals. The dress had a slit that went up high along one leg. Mom raised her eyebrows when she saw that.

The hostess led us through the whole huge restaurant, past tanks of fish and long scrolls and tables full of diners. As we approached each table, I tried to guess if it was the table with B.D. I wondered if he had the thick, glossy hair that my dad claims is the pride of the Wu family. But no, instead we went past the whole roomful of tables to the back of the restaurant, and into a hallway.

The hallway had several doors leading off of it. I was beginning to wonder whether the hostess was going to show us the bathrooms, when she stopped and opened a door.

"Cool!" said Kenny. "We get a private room."

The room had dark paneling and a big round table in the middle. The people in the room were laughing and talking, but when we walked in, they all stopped and looked at us. I ducked behind Mom — I hate that feeling of everyone staring at me.

"Steve!" One man stepped forward, calling my dad. He did *not* have the pride-of-the-Wu-family hair — he had a round, shiny, bald head.

"B.D. — it's been too long," said Dad. They hugged, thumping each other on the back. After Mom and B.D. shook hands, Dad introduced Regina. I held my breath and waited for *it*.

B.D.'s eyes bugged out. *"Na ma piao liang!"* he exclaimed. *So pretty!* He stepped backward, as if Regina's beauty actually took up room.

Regina blushed, but you'd think she'd be used to it by now. People can't help themselves, admiring her smooth pink-white skin and her long, thick eyelashes — *so unusual for a Chinese girl!* And yes, she has the Wu family hair, so silky and shiny that children reach up to stroke it. If you don't know the word for *pretty* in Chinese, you'd learn it soon enough hanging around Regina in a Chinese restaurant.

Kenny, who is four years younger than Regina and three years older than me, bent down and whispered, "Whaddya want to bet Dad mentions Mathwhiz when he introduces me." I rolled my eyes. Last year Kenny came in third in a statewide math contest; now he stays after school twice a week so that he can practice and become an even bigger math geek.

"This is Kenny," Dad said, putting a hand on Kenny's shoulder. Before Dad could say anything else, B.D. said, "The math genius! Of course! Have you started thinking about colleges?"

"Ummmm." Kenny looked around the room and started to drift away. I think he was looking for a place to hide. Kenny usually avoids sustained contact with adults.

"And of course, Lucy." Dad patted me on the head as if I were a dog. B.D. looked at me and smiled politely. I guess after exclaiming over Regina and Kenny he had run out of things to say.

All around the room, people were speaking Chinese. One group of ladies was involved in an excited conversation, their voices rat-a-tatting like machine guns. I grabbed Kenny by the elbow. "Don't leave me," I begged. I was terrified that someone might try to start a conversation with me. If we got past *How are you?* and *How old are you?* I was in deep trouble in the Chinese-speaking department. *Wo shi-yi sui*, I practiced in my mind. *I'm eleven.*

"Relax," said Kenny. He pulled out a huge paperback biography of Benjamin Franklin and slid into a chair. Once Kenny immerses himself in a book, there's no chance of a decent conversation, so I pretended to be fascinated by the carved chair I was sitting in. *Oooohhh, such nice carvings of flowers and leaves! What pretty wood!*

Luckily, a waiter showed up, and everyone took that as a signal to find a seat. At least Kenny would have to put his book away now and talk to me. The chairs around the table began to fill with people. I was glad that I had grabbed one next to Kenny.

I caught one of the rat-a-tat ladies giving me a funny look. Then she leaned over and said something to the person next to her, and she *pointed her chopsticks at me.* How rude! Before I could glare back at her, Regina tapped me on the shoulder.

"Lucy, get up. You need to change seats."

"Excuse me? You're not the boss of me." I turned away from her. *She* probably wanted to sit next to Kenny.

"I'm serious. *Get up.*" She was using that mean whisper that I'd seen mothers use with small children at the library.

I looked around the table. There were two empty seats left. I could see Regina's purse hanging from one, and there was one by the door next to another rat-a-tat lady.

"What is your problem?" I mean-whispered back.

Then I heard a gentle cough behind Regina. An old man was standing there—I think it was his birthday we were celebrating. He made a little wave with the back of his hand and said something. It looked like he was saying, *Don't worry about it.*

Regina shook her head, and then smiled pleasantly as she gripped my arm tightly and lifted me out of my chair with one hand. *Ouch!* Suddenly, I realized that everyone at the table was watching us.

I dropped my head and let Regina steer me toward the last empty chair. When the table began to rumble with conversation again, Regina said, "The chair farthest from the door is for the oldest person. Didn't you know that?"

Obviously I didn't know that. Regina, on the other hand, wasn't even in college yet, but it was like she practically majored in Being Chinese. Me? I just wanted a menu to hide my face. Maybe they had my favorite, orange beef.

We didn't get menus. Instead of asking what we wanted, the waiters just brought in a huge tureen of soup on a cart and starting serving bowl after bowl. At first I was excited, because I love wonton soup, but this soup turned out to have veiny green vegetables and big black mushrooms. While everyone else happily slurped down their soup, I pressed the back of my spoon into the soup so that I only scooped up the broth.

The waiters started to bring in a whole line of dishes, each one scarier than the last. A whole fish with dead eyes that stared at me. Baby octopus with tiny tentacles that I imagined tickling the insides of my mouth. There was one plate I would not have even figured out if Regina hadn't squealed, "Jellyfish! Yeah!" I heaped some plain white rice on my plate and began to eat it slowly. Slowly enough to last the whole meal.

Mom caught my eye and made a *mmm . . . yummy!* face. I scowled back.

Clank! The lady sitting next to me plopped two small oysters onto my plate. She seemed nicer than Mrs. Rude-Pointer, so I smiled as politely as I could and shook my head. This only seemed to encourage her. She plucked up an oyster and gulped down the slimy insides and then showed me the empty shell. I shuddered and ate another mouthful of rice.

To be fair, I'm kind of a picky eater. Everyone loves blueberries, but to me, they just look like tiny blue eyeballs. And milk? Don't get me started on milk.

"Ta hui jiang zhong-wen ma?" The oyster lady looked

at my parents and gestured toward me. I knew what that meant: She wanted to know if I could speak Chinese.

"*Ta tingzhe dong,*" Dad answered. *She understands what she hears.* This was being generous—I only understood a little bit.

At the other end of the table, Kenny was having a great time. Kenny eats anything and everything, and the old man who took my seat and the other woman sitting next to Kenny took turns heaping food on his plate, urging him to eat more.

B.D. leaned over and said something to Mom while tilting his head toward Regina, who was practically ruling over the table, enjoying her food and chatting in perfect Chinese. My mom beamed and said something back. And something else. And something more.

Even though I couldn't hear what she was saying exactly, she was undoubtedly telling him that Regina had won a full scholarship to Hamilton University, and she had won it because she had started the Chinese Culture and Language Society at school. Regina had single-handedly gotten the school to offer Chinese as a class, persuaded the PTA to buy Chinese language software, and brought dozens of speakers to school to discuss Chinese language, food, history, and culture. I could tell that Mom was about to induct one more person into the *Isn't Regina Wu Wonderful* Club.

At that moment, I really, really hated Regina and I really, really wanted a plate of lasagna.

The Oyster Lady now seemed to make it her personal mission to find me something to eat. She spooned some beef on my plate that looked promising, but it was so spicy it made my eyes water. Some tofu? The texture made me shudder. She lifted a thin pink slice of something onto my plate. It looked like ham, but at this point I was suspicious.

"*Zhi shi shenma?*" I asked in my best, politest Chinese. *What is this?*

"*Zhu er duo.*" She responded cheerfully, taking another slice for herself.

My brain started clicking. These words sounded familiar! Suddenly, I pictured the *Chinese Baby* video I used to watch ages ago. It had animals, colors, and parts of the body. Wait—*zhu* meant pig!

For the first time that evening I felt a little excited. Maybe I did know more Chinese than I thought. I smiled at the Oyster Lady and tried to remember what *er duo* meant. That sounded like a word from the video, too.

My stomach dropped. I remembered—the body parts section of the video. *Er duo* means ear. Pig ear? No. Thank. You.

I wrinkled my mouth shut and shook my head. I was so grossed out that I couldn't even eat the Peking duck she put on my plate, its crispy skin just waiting to crackle in my mouth. I took another bite of rice.

A waiter clattered into the room with another cart and began serving each person from a large, shallow bowl. Whatever it was, it must be something so good that they wanted to make sure everyone got one. I turned my head to see what it was, but too many people were leaning over their plates, blocking my view.

Plunk! The waiter dropped it on my plate with a soft thud. It was small and gray, no bigger than a deck of cards. It wasn't pretty, either, like some of the other dishes. It looked like bits of meat tacked together in one lump. What was this?

I leaned back in my chair, and that's when I stopped looking at the mystery lump as a bunch of parts. There was a head, body, and legs. It was a perfectly skinned and cooked frog.

The Oyster Lady leaned over and said her first words in English all night. "Like chicken!" She smiled widely.

Suddenly, I was very grateful that Regina had forced me to sit near the door. I jumped out of my seat and started running.

Where *was* that bathroom?

CHAPTER TWO

"I am soooo embarrassed," whined Regina as we sped down the highway, away from the Golden Lotus. "Could you *be* more mortifying, Lucy?"

I didn't answer her. I still felt hot and sweaty after throwing up what seemed like five pounds of rice. I pressed my cheek against the cool car window.

"You know, the Golden Lotus is one of the most famous Chinese restaurants in the country. A lot of people would kill to eat there. But you?" Regina raised her voice, pretending to be me. "Oooh! New food! It's *scaaaaary.*" She was extra mad because Mom made her leave before she could try the Peking honey bananas.

"Some of that food was a little unusual," Mom pointed out to Regina. "Though I wish you had spoken up a little sooner, Lucy."

Mom didn't understand. The choice between yelling across the table in English when everyone else was speaking Chinese or having everyone listen to my lurching, broken Chinese had not seemed that appealing.

"Some of that *unusual* food represented the best of Chinese cooking, how *every part* of an animal can be made into something incredibly delicious . . ." Regina went on.

That made me think of the frog. I grabbed my stomach and moaned.

Regina let out a little shriek. "You're not going to puke in the car, are you?"

I didn't really think I was going to get sick again, but for just one second, I wanted to. On Regina.

"Do I need to pull over, honey?" Dad yelled from the front of the van.

"No, I think I'm okay," I called back.

"I'll bet you wanted . . . let me guess . . . *lasagna*," accused Regina.

"No, I didn't," I lied, but I don't think she believed me. "What's wrong with lasagna?"

Regina's upper lip curved into a sneer. "You are *Chinese*. You are supposed to like *Chinese food*," she hissed. When attractive people make faces like that, they look even uglier than normal people would.

"I do like Chinese food," I told her, even though discussing food was making me slightly queasy. "There are plenty of dishes from Panda Café that are just fine with me, like their egg drop soup and chicken fried rice."

Regina rolled her eyes. "That's not *real* Chinese food. Panda Café cannot even begin to compare with the Golden Lotus."

"That's *your* opinion," I told her.

She sniffed. "It's an opinion backed by one of the world's greatest Chinese chefs. When Chef Yee came to my school for the Chinese Culture and Language Society, he mentioned the Golden Lotus. I don't believe he discussed Panda Café." Regina practically spat out the words *Panda Café*, as if they tasted bad in her mouth.

"Just get over yourself," I muttered to her.

"Girls," Dad said sharply from the driver's seat. "Enough."

"You're a *banana*, a *Twinkie*," Regina whispered.

"What are you talking about now?" For a second, I thought Regina was telling me to eat something.

"You're yellow on the outside, white on the inside. That's what you are."

Who did Regina think she was, telling me how or how not to be Chinese? I am sure there are people, maybe lots of people, in China who do not love eating pig's ears and other weird stuff, and no one ever calls them out and tells them that *they are not Chinese enough*.

"You know who I am, Regina? I'm someone who's getting her own room in a few weeks after a certain know-it-all moves out!" After Regina left for college, I was going to have an entire bedroom to myself for the first time, ever. I could decorate *all* the walls the way *I* wanted, instead of having to look at pictures of Regina's stupid friends. Plus, my best friend, Madison, and I were going to have the most incredible slumber party for our joint birthday party, and it was going to be in *my* room.

Regina's mouth twitched. "Oh, is that what you think?" she purred.

"Well, duh, you're leaving, so yes, that's what I think."

Regina leaned forward until our heads were almost touching. "Then, let's just say that it's really too bad you don't speak Chinese better. You might have learned some important information tonight."

She's bluffing, I thought. *She's just making something up to show how bad my Chinese is.* Yet, for a moment I held my breath and looked at Kenny to see if he could help. Unfortunately, Kenny had fallen asleep.

I looked out the window so that Regina wouldn't think she had gotten to me. I was going to have the perfect year once she was gone. I was going to have my own room, and I was finally going to be in sixth grade at Westgate, the oldest in the school, the best year. Someone heard that we might even get a dance this year.

When Regina goes, my life will be perfect, I chanted to myself. *When Regina goes.*

CHAPTER THREE

I SHOULD HAVE KNOWN SOMETHING WAS UP BECAUSE THE next day Mom made a big breakfast, with bacon and waffles and fruit salad. Usually we just have cereal, unless it's Christmas or someone's birthday.

Dad waited until Kenny had staggered down the stairs to join the rest of us. Kenny's not much of a morning person—he slumped at the table, blinking slowly. His hair looked like a black porcupine was attacking his head.

"So," said Dad, rubbing his hands together. "I have a special announcement to make. I am leaving for China next week."

My stomach dropped. Even though Dad had been to China many times, every trip made me nervous. China was so far away—it wasn't like he was flying to New York or Boston, or even Chicago or Los Angeles. If something happened in China, how could we ever find him?

"Do you have to?" I asked, knowing the answer.

"Yes, Lucy, I have to go for work, but there's also something else." Dad paused, enjoying the drama for a moment. "I just confirmed everything yesterday. I'll be bringing someone back with me. Po Po's sister— *Yi Po!*" He said it like a game show host, announcing a prize.

"Say that again?" said Kenny.

The room seemed to tilt.

"What are you talking about? Po Po doesn't have a sister," I said. Po Po, my mom's mom, had taken care of me every day after school until she died two years ago. We talked about everything. She had never mentioned a sister.

"It's complicated," Mom said. "I didn't know about this sister until Mom told me, right before she died. They never saw each other after they were little girls."

The Chinese part of my life just doesn't make sense sometimes. Like there are a bunch of women I call *ai yi*, which means aunt, and when I was little, I thought my mom had a ton of sisters. But they weren't my real aunts, they were just friends of my mom's.

Maybe this was something like that—they're saying she was my grandmother's sister, but she's not really.

"Okay . . . so, she's coming to visit, like when Aunt Lin and Naomi come to visit?" Naomi, my cousin, is three years older than I am—we see them a couple times a year.

"Kind of. It's a big deal to fly from China to the States, though, Lucy, so she'd stay longer than just a couple of days . . . and . . ." Mom paused. She and Dad glanced at each other.

". . . the only space we have for her is . . . um . . ." Mom slowed down, not finishing her sentence.

Suddenly, I put it all together. She was going to stay in *my* room.

Regina smirked at me from across the table. *I told you so.*

". . . but it will only be until Christmas—that's not so long, right?" Mom smiled at me, as if that made everything better. "Then she'll go visit Auntie Lin."

My room was disappearing. Going, going, gone.

"What? Only if *eternity* is a week-long vacation," I said. "You can't do this to me. I'm supposed to have my own room, remember?" Today was August 10. I was wearing shorts and a T-shirt. By Christmas I would be wearing sweaters and jeans. And be twelve, not eleven. And practically halfway through sixth grade. Basketball season would have started.

This was a long, long time.

"I know you're disappointed," Mom started.

"That's an understatement," I said, pushing away from the table. I swallowed hard, pushing down the tears that were threatening to come up. "Thanks a lot for including me in this life-changing decision."

"There was no decision to make," Dad said. "She's family. It's an honor for us to have her come visit. End of story. I got word yesterday that her paperwork was finalized." Dad gave me a look that meant *end of discussion*.

"Yeah, Lucy," chimed in Regina. "We're Chinese. We honor and value our elders. We don't think about whether we get our own room." She looked at Dad and plastered on an extra big, aren't-I-wonderful smile. Dad nodded approvingly. Regina is such a kiss-up.

"We're Chinese-*American*," I snapped. "And this *American* would like her own room!"

I grabbed my basketball and went outside to play in the driveway. I was too mad to talk—I needed some hoop therapy. After a couple of dribbles, I faked a pass to the left, whirled around, and went for a top-of-the-key jumper. *Lucy Wu goes in for the buzzer-beater!* The ball thudded off the backboard. No basket.

When I tell people that I play basketball, I usually get two kinds of reactions. The first is an awkward pause while my entire height of four-foot-nothing gets examined up one side and down the other, followed by something like, "O-kaaaay. What other sports do you like?" The second, while more positive, is really not any better. It's a big fishy grin, followed by, "Oh! Just like Yao Ming!" Like I have anything in common with a seven-and-a-half-foot-tall male basketball player, other than the fact that we're both Chinese.

But I love basketball. The day I got the hang of dribbling the ball through my legs counts as one of the best days of my life, and that feeling I get when I *know* the ball's going in because everything has lined up perfectly is the greatest rush. To me, getting the ball to an open teammate on a no-look pass is a thing of beauty. And tell me there's something more exciting than the last few seconds of a tied-up basketball game where *tenths* of a second count.

I crouched down, eyed the basket, and fired again. This time the ball went in.

"Hey! Luce! Get me the rebound!" I turned around even though I knew who it was.

Madison Jameson and I have been best friends for five years, ever since we snuck out of ballet class to watch a pickup basketball game outside. We've been playing together on a league team ever since then, and we have our whole lives planned out. After playing varsity hoops for all four years in high school, we're going to the University of Tennessee so we can play basketball for Pat Summitt. Just about every person who has played for

Pat Summitt has played in the Final Four, the legend-ary best-of-the-best round of the national tourney, and they've won the women's championship more times than anybody. After *we* win *our* NCAA tournament, Madison and I will play professional ball in the WNBA for a few years, and then open a design store for girls who love sports. No frilly pink princessy stuff, but not boy stuff, either. Just cool stuff, like lockers to hold your sports equipment and specially designed boards to record your team schedules and workout routines. We're going to call it At the Buzzer.

"C'mon." Madison snapped her fingers impatiently. "Move that ball!" She sounded just like Coach Mike, the coach of our team, the Inferno.

I snagged the ball and whipped it to her. Madison grabbed the ball and went in for a layup. The ball went in. It must be nice to be the tallest girl in the class.

"What's up? You doing your fifty?" asked Madison. Coach Mike had told us to do fifty free throws every day during the summer. Free throws can make or break a game, he says.

"Not exactly. My life just exploded." I told her the news. Madison's eyes widened. Madison doesn't have surprise relatives from foreign countries. Her family practically came over on the *Mayflower*.

"I guess we better hurry up and decorate your room, huh?" she asked. Madison and I had been talking all summer about how we would redecorate my room once Regina was gone. We like the same colors—violet and ice blue.

"Yeah—maybe we can go to Sharpe's soon," I said. I didn't feel very enthusiastic. Knowing I was getting a roommate was taking out the fun.

Madison poked me. "Cheer up. I have some news."

"What?"

"Mom says the class assignments are out. We're in the same class!" Madison's mom volunteered at the school, so Madison was always the first to know what was going on.

That *was* good news. I don't think I could stand it if we weren't in the same class. Certain kids never get to be in the same class, like Paul Terry and Jamie

Watkins, because they are troublemakers. "Who'd we get?" I asked.

"Some new teacher, Ms. Phelps. Mom didn't know much about her."

"Who is in our class?"

"Let me think . . . Steven, Nate, Anil, Rick, and Andrew . . . Haley, Anne, Serena, and Lauren . . . Alexa, Oscar . . ." Madison's voice trailed off.

"Anyone else? From our class last year?" I tried to sound casual, but I was pretty sure I had yelped. *Please say he's in our class.*

"Who am I forgetting? Oh, yes, Talent, of course."

"Oh." I sighed. Talent Chang. Everyone seems to think we should be friends because we're both Chinese, short, and in the same grade. The resemblance ends there, though. She dresses, acts, and talks like an annoying miniature adult. There's a rumor that when her family moved here from Taiwan, her parents made her watch public television until she learned English.

"Lucy, be nice."

"*You* be nice," I retorted. I lined up on the crack that acted as my free-throw line and shot the ball. The ball swirled in the hoop and then fell out.

"*Now* I remember who else is in our class," said Madison.

"Really? Who?" Oops. I sounded a little too enthusiastic.

"That new kid from last year. What's his name? Oh, yeah, Harrison Miller."

"Oh, okay." I bit my lip to keep from shrieking. Even Madison didn't know about my crush on Harrison Miller, and I planned to keep it that way, at least for a while. When Harrison moved here last year, some kids nicknamed him Mr. California Cool. He wore his hair long, and a necklace with a little carved dolphin. Some of the other boys, like Jamie Watkins, tried to tease him, but it just seemed to slide right off him. Haley, who was assigned to Harrison's lunch table last year, said he was a vegetarian and didn't eat just peanut butter and jelly all the time, like when Andrew tried being a vegetarian for two weeks. Harrison ate stuff like brown rice with lentils and cashews.

Other kids thought this was weird. I didn't.

Suddenly, I wondered how long I had been daydreaming about Harrison. And whether Madison knew that I was thinking about him. I started dribbling the ball again.

"Listen, I gotta go," said Madison. She lived two blocks away, on the other side of the street. "Call me later, Leaping Wombat?" This was our private joke: We made up names according to our initials.

"See you, Magenta Jelly," I said. As I watched her walk away, Regina came out and dumped two garbage bags full of clothes in front of me.

"Mom says that we need to start cleaning up the house for Yi Po. You need to go inside and help clean out the basement." If Regina's favorite thing is to give orders, her second favorite thing to do is give orders on behalf of Mom and Dad.

"I'm still playing ball," I said, holding the ball on my

hip. "And you need to move those clothes out of my way."
I poked the bag with my foot.

"Mom said *now*," said Regina.

I tried to give the ball one good thump, so Regina and the whole world would know I was still mad, but instead of bouncing high in the air, the ball hit an old shoe, flew back, and hit me in the knee. Even my own ball had turned against me.

CHAPTER FOUR

THERE WAS ONE THING REGINA HADN'T FIGURED OUT while she was busy enjoying the fact that I wasn't getting my own room. If Dad was going to China, he wasn't taking *her* to college. Suddenly, honoring our elders wasn't at the top of Regina's list, either.

"He could wait," she whined on her cell phone. "He could wait a couple of days until his *first child* goes to college." Her eyes were red and her nose made a terrible snoggy sound. So much for *piao liang*.

"Big baby," I said as she laid out her sob story for the umpteenth time.

Regina scowled and stuck her tongue out at me. She managed to do this without skipping a beat on her phone call.

Even though Regina was acting all neglected, Mom and Dad couldn't seem to say a sentence without including her name. Should Regina sign up for the linen service, or should we buy her more towels? Regina, do you need anything from Sharpe's? Does Regina need new clothes? (Regina stopped whining long enough to say yes, she did.)

Regina, Regina, Regina. I was so sick of her! And her stuff, too. She had somehow managed to take over our entire room with her packing. I couldn't wait for her to leave.

One day I walked into the room we shared and discovered Regina folding a quilt into a big plastic bin. *My* quilt. Her quilt was now on my bed. I knew immediately what was going on. Even though our quilts look similar, hers is seven years older and it's a bit more worn.

"Regina! What are you doing with my flower quilt?" The quilts were special, made by Po Po. Each quilt had a green border with flowers growing toward the middle, so that it looked like a garden. I could still picture her working on the quilt, patiently stitching flower after flower until she thought it looked just right. For a long time, I didn't even want to wash it because I could still smell all the things that reminded me of Po Po—her lavender and chamomile soap, the slightly mothbally smell of her sweaters, a little Tiger Balm.

Regina threw her hands in the air. "I knew you'd say something like that, Lucy!" she said, as if this were my fault. "I'm going to *college*, okay? I have to take nice things because I'm making all new friends and I can't go around with a ratty quilt." I looked at her. She tried a different approach. "C'mon, Luce, *pleeease*? I really want something from home that's special. It's bad enough Daddy won't be there."

My mom walked in at that point. "Ma! Can you tell Lucy that I need her quilt at school? It's nicer than mine," Regina pleaded.

Mom rubbed her hands over her face. "I can't believe your dad is taking another trip," she said, more to herself than to us. "Regina, honey, it's Lucy's quilt. You can take your quilt, or find something else from home."

I made a face at Regina from where Mom couldn't see me. *So there.*

"Fine! I can see that no one cares about me!" Regina

cried. She picked up the quilt to throw it at me, but part of the quilt caught on the edge of the metal bed frame. We all heard an awful *rrriiippp*, and suddenly I could see the batting through a gash in the quilt. *My* quilt.

"Look at what you did! I might be a banana, but at least I'm not a selfish brat!" I screamed at Regina. My words burned my throat. Regina, for once, had nothing to say, in Chinese or English. She looked at me with wide eyes and let the quilt fall to the floor in a pile.

I scooped up the quilt in my arms and buried my face in it. How could she? Out of all the rotten things Regina had ever done, this was the worst. Mom put her arm around me, saying she was sorry and that we could probably fix it. But that wasn't the point—it wouldn't be the same as when Po Po made it. Now it was ugly, damaged. I wasn't just not having the perfect year anymore—it had become downright horrible.

I ran to Kenny's room, too choked up to say anything. Kenny let me sit on his bed until Regina finished packing.

● ● ●

MOM FELT PRETTY BAD ABOUT THE QUILT — BAD ENOUGH that she invited Madison over for dinner when Dad said he had to work late to get ready for his trip. Regina disappeared with some friends.

"Nothing fancy," Mom warned Madison, "but you'll have a lot of leftovers to choose from." Mom wasn't kidding. When we sat down to dinner, we had half a quiche, Caesar salad, green beans, two hot dogs, sesame noodles, almost a whole container of General Tso's chicken from Panda Café, and my favorite, *bao zi*, which is Chinese for yummy steamed bun with a delicious ground pork center.

"Try this," I said to Madison, putting one of the *bao zi* on her plate. "Dip it in some soy sauce."

Madison took a bite. "Pretty good!" she said. "What is this? A Chinese hamburger?"

"They're called *bao zi*," said Mom. "Though I think your name for it is pretty good, too." They smiled at each other. My mom and Madison have always gotten along really well, sometimes even better than Mom and me.

"Take more," urged Mom. "There's plenty without Regina and Mr. Wu here."

"No Regina," I cheered. "More food, more fun."

Mom pulled out her favorite line. "You two are sisters and one day . . ."

"I know, I know. One day, we'll be the *beeeeeessst* of friends," I finished for her. Fat chance, especially after the quilt.

"You're lucky," Mom reminded me. "Po Po never got to be friends with her sister."

Well, there goes a perfectly good dinner. I pushed back my plate with the *bao zi* still on it. I wasn't hungry anymore.

Madison, however, seemed to perk up at the mention of Yi Po. She took another bite of her *bao zi*, and said, "Po Po never got to be friends with her sister? Yi Po? Did she talk about her at all?"

For a second, I felt mad at Madison. If I didn't want to think about Yi Po, then she shouldn't, either. But I had to admit, it was a good question.

Mom made a sweeping motion with her hands, clearing the space in front of her. "No, she didn't. It kind of came out of the blue. She'd been in the hospital for several days, really out of it, and then one day, she sat up in the hospital bed and said, 'Nancy, I have something to tell you. I want to tell you about my family's trip to America.'"

I knew the story, and knew Madison did, too. When we were little, we used to beg Po Po to tell us the story over and over. She made coming to New York from China sound magical—the subways and the five-and-dime stores. We always laughed when she told us her first words in English: *ice cream*, *balloon*, and *paper doll*.

Mom took a long breath and blew it out slowly. "I know you know the story, the one she liked to tell. But this time she told a different story. She talked about the things she never liked to talk about: her father dying suddenly in their apartment, and how she and her mother became stuck in the U.S. after the attack on Pearl Harbor."

When Po Po told her story, she always made this part the shortest. She would say, "Then, after my father died . . ." But this was just what I was afraid of with my dad traveling to China—something happening to him in a faraway place.

Mom stared at the empty space she had made in front of herself. "I knew that my grandmother and mother had to work in a warehouse, cleaning, just to make some money. What I didn't know was that they had to go to dozens of places to look for work, because people refused to hire them, thinking they were Japanese. Some people spat on them, and called them 'dirty Japs.'"

Po Po had never made the warehouse sound like a bad place. When she told me about it, she always made it sound wonderful, because it was the place where she and her mother met Joe Fong, the man who would become her stepfather. But now I realized she must have been covering up: A warehouse was probably not a great place for a kid.

Mom sat up and gripped the edge of the table. "Then Po Po reached over and grabbed me from where I was

39

sitting next to the bed. 'It was all supposed to be temporary, you know!' she shouted. 'We were supposed to go back!' "

My heart sped up, as though Po Po herself had shouted at me. My grandmother had never raised her voice at me, not once in my whole life.

"I started patting her, trying to soothe her. 'Yes, Ma, I know. You couldn't go back, because of the war, and then you all met Joe.' I couldn't figure out why she was so upset. Didn't she have a good life in the U.S.? Hadn't she been happy all these years?"

I was so lost in the story, thinking of my grandmother, that I had forgotten where we were going on this journey of memories. But Madison remembered the destination.

"She wanted to go back because . . ." started Madison, but Mom interrupted.

"Because there was another daughter, Po Po's little sister. They had left her in China." For a moment I felt swept away by those words. *Another daughter.* If Regina and I had been the girls in this story, *another daughter* would have been me. "At first I thought I had misunderstood, but Po Po was too specific. Her sister had been two years younger, and they had left her with an aunt to care for her until they came back."

Mom blinked. "I don't know why she never made it to the States. I can guess. There was so much going on in China then. War, famine, the Japanese invasion." She took a drink of water and looked at me. "I gathered that your grandmother's mother tried to find her for a long time, but her letters were never answered, and they assumed the worst. But they never forgot. Your grandmother never forgot her sister."

"Then why didn't Po Po ever tell me about her? Why did she wait so long to tell you?" I asked. I didn't want to know this about my grandmother, that she lived with such a sad secret. I didn't want this to dilute all the happy memories I had, the good ones.

"I don't know why she didn't tell us earlier, Lucy," said Mom. "Maybe it was just too sad for her to talk about. I think that at the end, she realized the secret would disappear with her if she didn't say anything."

Mom laced her fingers together and rested her chin on the little bridge.

"But how could anyone *not know* what happened to her?" I demanded. Maybe if someone had known, Yi Po would not be coming to the States now.

"*Lucy,*" Kenny interrupted impatiently. While we had been talking, Kenny had quietly devoured the quiche, a hot dog, and most of the General Tso's chicken. "Don't you know anything? China was a mess back then. You know how the U.S. had the Civil War? North versus South? China had one, too, when Po Po was little."

When Kenny talks about history, you can't help listening to him. He gets so excited—and Kenny doesn't get excited about much.

"The Nationalists fought the Communists for control of China until the Japanese invaded. The Japanese were brutal, killing millions of Chinese, so then the two groups joined together. Once they drove out the Japanese, they starting fighting each other again. The war lasted over twenty years. And all that time, people had to literally run for their lives, from the fighting, the soldiers. It wouldn't have been hard to lose track of someone."

Mom gave Kenny a wide-eyed look, possibly because ever since Kenny turned fourteen, he usually spoke in three-word grunts in front of her. "How do you know all this, Kenny?"

Kenny stopped and stared at her, as if he just remembered she was there. "Books," he said, and shoveled a forkful of salad into his mouth.

"So, Mr. Wu went to China to look for her on one of his business trips?" asked Madison.

Mom shook her head. "He didn't go looking for her. You'll have to get Mr. Wu to tell you the whole story. All I can say is, noodles were involved."

Noodles? What did that mean?

Madison smiled at me. "Isn't it incredible that she lived through all of that and is coming to visit? She's finally getting reunited with her family," she said. Apparently Madison had forgotten who was getting the short end of this deal.

"Yeah," I agreed sarcastically. "Maybe if I'm really lucky there will be a long-lost brother, and *he'll* come, too."

THAT NIGHT, THOUGHTS ABOUT YI PO AS A LITTLE KID kept popping into my head. I couldn't imagine what it would be like. What if I had been separated from Kenny and Regina? It would be weird to know that I had a brother and sister, but not really *know* them—the way I know that Kenny can recite all the area codes for every major city in the country, or that Regina hates pulpy orange juice.

Mom had said Po Po's sister was younger. Maybe she was too little to remember Po Po.

I heard a thump in the hallway and peeked out the door. Dad was getting his big suitcase out of the hall closet.

"Hey, *Mei Mei*," whispered Dad. *Mei Mei* means little sister. "Shouldn't you be asleep?"

"Yeah, I guess," I said. "Lots to think about."

Mom had gone to sleep awhile ago. A light glowed from beneath Kenny's door, but we could hear him snoring. Regina was still out with her friends.

Dad pointed at his briefcase leaning against the wall. "Am I getting a surprise package for this trip?"

"Da-a-a-ad." That was something I did when I was little. I used to put stuffed animals and drawings in his briefcase. I even let him take Matilda, my stuffed mouse, once for good luck.

"Oh, come on," said Dad. "It's a long trip. Matilda would make great company."

A nervous shiver shot up through me. *Long trip.* Why couldn't I have one of those dads who worked from home?

"You can have Matilda," I said. "But I have a better idea." I tiptoed downstairs and got a couple of DVDs and a magazine. I ran back upstairs and grabbed Matilda.

"No peeking," I told him. I put everything in his briefcase. "It's a new and improved surprise package." Dad grinned.

"Thanks, *Mei Mei*," said Dad. "Now I'm sure to have a great trip."

Making the surprise package took away some of the shaky feeling. Now I just wished that I could tear Dad's trip in half. I wanted him to come home soon—but I didn't want *her* to come with him.

CHAPTER FIVE

DAD LEFT IN A TAXI EARLY IN THE MORNING. I DIDN'T get up but I thought I heard the taxi door slam shut. I tried to ignore the fluttery feeling in my chest.

When I finally did get out of bed, I looked over at Regina, who was still sleeping. Her hair spilled across her pillow and her face was gentle and soft. She actually looked *nice*. For the last few days, I had been so mad at Regina for tearing my quilt that I had barely spoken to her. Now, I wished for the old days, when Regina acted like I was the one who was special, making me little presents and bragging about my basketball to her friends.

Regina sat up and rubbed her eye. "Hey," she said.

"Hey yourself," I said.

"Is Daddy gone?"

"Yeah. I heard the taxi this morning." It was weird to start talking again after giving her the silent treatment.

There was a pause, and then we both said, "I wish he didn't have to go." We laughed.

Regina patted her bed. "Come here a sec, Lucy."

I walked over slowly. When I was younger, when we first started sharing a room, I couldn't wait for morning, when Regina would call me over to her bed. She would pull the covers over us and we would pretend to be stowaways on a ship or orphans hiding from bad guys in a cave. I couldn't remember the last time we had done that. I leaned on the side of her bed, both feet planted firmly on the floor.

Regina sat up and pulled up her knees under the sheets, forming a smooth pink mountain. She pulled her arms around herself and took in a quick breath.

"Lucy—I'm sorry. I'm really, really sorry I tore your quilt."

I don't know where tears come from, but somewhere I was having a rush order of them. Not little trickly ones, either, but great big gushers. I think it was because I could tell from the way she spoke that Regina knew exactly what I was feeling—it was more than the quilt. It was missing Po Po and knowing that there would be no other quilt from her.

Regina gave me a hug. "You know that if I could take it back, I would—don't you? I would give anything to take back what I did."

I nodded. "I know."

Regina was crying, too, now. "I still miss her, you know. We all do."

"I wish there was more to remember her by . . . I'm so scared that if I lose something, or forget something, that one day there won't be anything left," I said.

I closed my eyes and tried to think of five things about Po Po. She sang along with the radio when she drove. She loved peach cobbler with vanilla ice cream. Her fingernails were always perfect ovals. She kept little dishes of treats all around the house. On my eighth birthday, she and Regina decorated my birthday cake to look like a basketball court. I loved that cake, even though the hoops threatened to crash into the icing the whole time they were singing "Happy Birthday."

I thought of something to say to Regina—something to make her happy. "I think Po Po would have been proud of you for starting the Chinese club and getting that scholarship."

Regina smiled, her cheeks squeezing out a few more tears. "You think so? She had gotten so sick by the time the club was really taking off."

"Definitely. What did she used to say? About the frog?" For a second I panicked. I couldn't remember what she said exactly, just the vague murmur of her voice.

"She said 'don't be a frog at the bottom of a well'— *jing di zhi wa*. The frog in the well thinks he has life so great, but all he knows is the well. He doesn't know what the ocean is like. Think of greater things you can achieve." As soon as Regina said it, I could hear my grandmother's voice again, cheering us on.

It felt as though Regina and I had been on a seesaw for a long time, up and down, back and forth, trying to get the upper hand or avoid being on the bottom. Now we had reached a point of perfect balance. No one was higher or lower—we were just right.

● ● ●

A FEW DAYS LATER, MOM, KENNY, AND I DROVE REGINA to school, three hours away. The car was so full that Kenny and I had to rest our feet on bags *and* hold boxes on our laps. *Then* we found out we had to schlep Regina's stuff up four flights of stairs.

"Couldn't you have gotten a room on a lower floor?" asked Kenny as we looked up the long flights of stairs. "Or gone to a school that's heard of elevators?"

We spent the whole afternoon carrying Regina's stuff up the stairs, though by the end a small herd of guys in Regina's dorm was helping us. All hoping, undoubtedly, for a chance to talk to Regina. By the time Mom, Kenny, and I left for our hotel, Regina already had plans for breakfast, lunch, and dinner the next day.

We stuck around for another day so Mom could go to a bunch of boring parent meetings, and then we drove home. Before we left, Regina pulled me aside and handed me a box.

Inside, there was a beautiful silver snowflake pendant on a red ribbon, in honor of my middle name, Mengxue, or Snow Dream. When she was six, Regina had a dream about finding a laughing baby in a basket by a snow-covered forest. She told my mom about the dream, and a few days later, Mom found out she was pregnant with me. When I was born, Mom decided that Mengxue would be my Chinese name.

I turned around and lifted up my hair so Regina could tie the ribbon around my neck. Then we hugged good-bye.

"Thank you," I said. "Watch out for those boys."

"Be good," she said.

Regina could be bossy, selfish, and annoying. Her grades gave my parents unrealistic expectations about mine. She always hogged the closet, took too long in the bathroom, and nagged me about cleaning up my half of the room. But I was going to miss her.

CHAPTER SIX

IN A FEW DAYS, MY FAMILY HAD GONE FROM FIVE TO three, and the house felt strangely big. Mom, Kenny, and I rattled around inside, like marbles in a coffee can. When Mom went back to work, Kenny was in charge now that Regina was gone. This was kind of a joke since Kenny lives in his own world. He's always reading one fat book or another, and when he's not doing that, he's losing things. Mom and Dad say this is because Kenny is a math genius. I say it's because he's a space cadet, and I'm tired of helping him look for his jacket/keys/homework/right shoe before school.

On Saturday, Mom took Madison and me to Sharpe's so we could get started on the great room-decorating project. While I wasn't going to get to enjoy the room as *all* mine, as Madison pointed out, I was going to be living in it, so why not have something nice? We also had to buy school supplies—that was the deal we struck with Mom.

We decided to go to the school supply section first. It was wall-to-wall moms and kids digging through bins of markers, pencils, glue sticks, scissors, and notebooks. One little kid had found a space on the floor for a tantrum. "I wanted *THAT ONE*!" he screamed, pointing at another little boy who must have been holding the last Spider-Man pencil box.

Madison and I looked at the school supply list. "C'mon," she said, pulling on my arm. "We'll start at one end of this mess and work our way across. You check off the items as we find them."

Together, we found the number-two pencils, ballpoint pens, index cards, highlighters, red felt-tip pens, three-ring binders, wide-rule paper, and pocket folders. We were picking out dividers when a voice rang out. "Madison! Lucy! Don't get those dividers! They don't have reinforced holes."

We should have done school supplies later.

At the end of the report folder aisle stood Talent Chang, steering a cart overflowing with school supplies. A huge econopack of tape was preparing to fall off the top of a mountain of colored pencils and manila folders. "Hey, Talent," said Madison cheerily.

Talent picked up a different package of dividers and put it in our cart. "Get this brand. They're much better."

"Wow!" I said sarcastically. "Thank goodness you saved us from inferior notebook dividers."

Talent looked at me. "You're welcome. Don't you hate it when they rip?"

Madison elbowed me gently. "Are you shopping for school supplies, too?" she asked.

"I'm not shopping for myself, of course. I finished that shopping as soon as the school list became available," said Talent. I imagined her breathlessly checking the school website until the supply list was posted. "I'm here with my parents. They're helping start a Chinese school." She looked at me. "It's going to be on Saturday mornings. You should come."

Chinese school? On Saturday mornings?

"No way! That's when we have basketball practice!" Last year, we had come within one game of going to regionals. I was determined that we were going to make it this year.

"Lucy," Talent said, "Chinese school is much more important than basketball."

"Whoa," said Madison. "You really think so?"

"Basketball is *fun*," I said.

"Having the ability to converse with millions of people is also fun," countered Talent.

"Maybe you don't really understand basketball. Have you ever been in the gym when there's ten seconds left and the teams are tied?" asked Madison. Madison, being nicer than me, actually seemed concerned that Talent didn't understand basketball.

"Don't you want to be part of a culture that has lasted thousands of years?" Talent asked me.

"When you need Chinese to play basketball, come talk to me," I said.

Talent ignored my comment. "The school won't be just about language. The Chinese school curriculum will cover significant cultural events, handicrafts, food . . .

though, come to think of it, are you even fluent in Mandarin?" She squinted, like she could tell by looking at me.

If she says that I need help on how to be Chinese, I'm going to wrap those eight rolls of tape around her mouth. "Well, it sounds *super* exciting, but no thanks," I told her.

"I think you'll be sorry," said Talent, frowning. "I'll see you Tuesday."

"See you, Talent," said Madison. I didn't even bother saying good-bye. After we watched her leave, Madison sighed. "Feeling rude today?"

It's different for you, I wanted to say. Instead, I said, "Can you believe she said Chinese school was more important than *basketball*?" I figured Madison had to agree with that.

"Okay, yeah, that was something," agreed Madison. "But she's entitled to her opinion. And why does it have to be one or the other, anyway? Can't they both be important?"

"Not if they're both on Saturday morning!" I declared.

"I can't be at basketball practice and Chinese school at the same time."

"Anyway," said Madison. "You could still be nice to her. I think sometimes she's kind of insecure under all that bossiness."

"And under all my rudeness is a real and true desire to play ball, which Talent shouldn't mess with. She can take her insecurities out on someone else."

"Speaking of someone else," said Madison. "Should we worry . . ."

She didn't have to finish her sentence. As I glanced over to the linens department, I saw it. Talent was talking to my mom.

MADISON AND I SCOURED EVERY DEPARTMENT, EVERY inch of Sharpe's. We were looking for stuff to decorate my room, but I was also hiding from Mom. I wanted to delay the moment the words came out of her mouth. *Chinese school. You should go to Chinese school.*

Mom caught up with us in the pet supplies aisle. She

didn't even ask what we were doing there, since neither one of us has a pet. She just started right in.

"Isn't it wonderful? A Chinese school, right here in town," Mom said. "Your friend Talent told me all about it."

I didn't know what part of her statement to argue about first. Whether Talent was my friend or whether Chinese school was a great idea.

"Yeah, some friend. What friend wants you to go to school on Saturdays?" I said.

"Lucy . . ." Mom warned.

"And, anyway, I can speak some Chinese."

"It's passable," said Mom, "but we don't speak much Chinese around the house, and this would be a great way to improve during Yi Po's visit."

"Mom, it's at the same time as basketball practice. Saturday mornings, remember?"

"We-e-e-llll . . ." When Mom said a word like that, she usually was about to introduce a plan that she knew I would not like. "Maybe you could just skip this season and give Chinese school a try. Then we'll look at things again in the spring."

Yeah, I knew what that meant. It meant that this spring, the argument would be *You've already missed a season, why don't you just stick with Chinese school?*

"Mom, I really, really, really don't want to go to Chinese school." Mom looked at me. "I *have* to play basketball." *I have to breathe. I have to drink water.*

"Let's see what Daddy says when he gets home," Mom suggested cheerily.

It was a long shot, admittedly, but better than nothing. I closed my eyes and sent a mental message to Dad in China. *You're my last hope, Dad. Don't let me down!*

CHAPTER SEVEN

"If I do say so myself, it looks awesome," said Madison.

I had to agree. As I looked around my redecorated bedroom, I thought it was just as good as any of the makeover shows.

Madison had come up with the great idea of decorating around my middle name, Snow Dream. With Kenny's and Mom's help, we had painted the walls a cool pale blue. Mirrors in different sized circles were stuck to the wall to look like falling snow, and my stuffed animals were now dressed in scarves and hats. Madison's mom had even let us have an old pair of Madison's white leather ice skates, and we propped them up on my bookshelf. The only thing that really didn't look quite right was my bed, which still had the old quilt on it, now with a bumpy seam where Mom tried to fix it. Mom wasn't about to earn her Girl Scout badge for sewing anytime soon.

Now I was sitting on my bed, cutting out snowflake after snowflake and tying string to each one. Madison was standing on the stepladder, hanging them from the ceiling.

"We should take pictures, so that when we're rich and famous, we'll have a picture of our first decorating project," said Madison.

"So rich, and so famous," I agreed, putting on what we called our *la-di-da* accent.

"Oh, *dahling*," said Madison. "Did you hear? Pat Summitt wants us to decorate her home after we've finished here. She saw this room and said that it was just fabulous."

I giggled. "Oh, I just don't know, *dahling*. We're just so very busy . . . and *fabulous*."

I cracked up. We couldn't stop using the word *fabulous* while we hung up more and more snowflakes from the ceiling. "Could you pass the tape? It's *fabulous*!" "Isn't this new wall color *fabulous*?" "Your shampoo smells *fabulous*!"

Kenny walked by the room. "Kenny! You look *fabulous*!" Madison shouted. This made us laugh harder.

He poked his head in. "Man, you guys are weird." He shook his head and looked up at the ceiling. "Uhhhh—did you make sure that it was okay to put up *all* of these snowflakes?"

We stopped and looked around. Maybe we had gotten a little carried away. Once we had figured out how to hang the snowflakes using a pole and some double-sided tape, we couldn't stop. My room had gone from Winter Wonderland to Blinding Blizzard.

"Normally, I don't think Mom would care, but with Yi Po coming and all . . ." Kenny shrugged. "It's up to you."

"It's no big deal," said Madison quickly, glancing at me. "We'll just take a couple down." Kenny had popped the bubble, deflating all our silliness.

For a moment, I had forgotten Yi Po was coming and was taking over half of my beautiful new room. She would be here in four days, right after school started. I began ripping down the snowflakes.

● ● ● ●

I DECIDED TO THROW MYSELF INTO GETTING READY FOR school. I finished the assignments that I had been putting off all summer. I read *Number the Stars,* the book that had been assigned for reading, answered the questions on the worksheet, and I even proofread my answers. Mom and I went shopping for new sneakers and a new backpack.

I think even kids who don't usually like school look forward to the first day of school. The teachers are in a good mood, everything is new, and there are friends to catch up with. For the first day of school, Madison and I agreed, dress nicely, but don't look like you're trying too hard. I picked a white polo with thin, light blue stripes and a matching blue skirt. Madison had to drop off a form at the main office, so I waited for her in front of the big glass trophy case at the main entrance. Class started in five minutes.

"Hey, Lucy!" Serena and Haley came over to me. "What's up?"

"Just waiting for Madison. How was your summer?"

"Too busy. I went to debate camp, sailing camp, French immersion camp, and intensive math camp. School will be a nice break." Haley was an only child and always had about a million things going on. She had also been our class president for the last three years.

"I finally did a back tuck!" Serena was a gymnast and had been one since kindergarten. When she got excited, she bounced up and down until her knees were practically at chin level.

"How was your summer?" Haley asked.

I thought of saying, *My family and Talent Chang have wrecked the best year of my life*, but decided that might be too much of a downer on the first day of school. "It was okay, not great."

"Well, cheer up!" Serena put an arm around me. "This year we're going to rule the school!"

This was true. In spite of everything that was going on, being a sixth grader was something that could *not* be taken away from me. There was no denying that sixth grade was the best year at school. I watched a sobbing kindergartner walking by with her mom, and thought how sixth graders seemed like giants, practically adults, when I was that little.

Madison showed up. "Hi, guys! What's up? Any word if we're having a dance this year?"

Before Serena and Haley could answer, the warning bell rang. We started walking to our room, and over the ringing, I heard Haley ask:

"So, do you know anything about this new teacher, Ms. Phelps?"

Ms. PHELPS IS TWENTY-NINE YEARS OLD AND HAS A BOY-friend who is a semi-professional baseball player. She has two cats, drives a purple VW, and loves red shoes. This is her fourth year teaching. Her first name is Carla.

We found this out playing one of those get-to-know-you games in our first class. I decided that I really liked her because she included herself in the game *and* she let us sit wherever we wanted. Madison and I chose desks next to each other, and Harrison was two rows in front of us—good for sneaking peeks.

I also had to give her points for a nice-looking class-room. The windows were lined with leafy ferns in terra-cotta planters. There was a reading nook in one corner with a rug, beanbags, and a bookcase topped with an aquarium. She also had posters of the Swiss Alps, the Grand Canyon, and a rocky coast with a lighthouse. She said that she hoped beautiful places would inspire us.

At lunchtime, I grabbed the end of a long table so that Madison, Serena, Haley, and I could sit together. I saw Talent looking for a place to sit, too, but I looked away. Every time she came near me, it was like Chinese school was getting closer.

"Ms. Phelps seems nice," said Haley. Madison nodded in agreement.

"She doesn't seem like a yeller," added Serena.

"Oh, yeah! Remember last year? Ms. Pendergast?" Andrew leaned over from the next table to join the conversation. *"I will not tolerate this behavior for one more minute!"* He narrowed his eyes and snarled in a perfect imitation.

Madison winced at the memory.

"Yeah, but would you rather have someone like that substitute we had last year at Christmas? The college guy?" Lauren called from the end of the table. Lauren loved to play Would You Rather? For my money, at least Ms. Pendergast seemed to care, while the college guy just wrote our assignments on the board and spent most of his time checking his cell phone.

"College guy," agreed Madison and Serena.

"Ms. Pendergast," said Haley.

"Pendergast," chimed in Andrew.

"What about you, Lucy?" asked Lauren. "C'mon, be the tiebreaker."

I opened my mouth to answer when Harrison suddenly appeared next to me. "What's up? Can I vote?" he asked. Harrison. Harrison Miller. With the cutest smile. His long dark hair fell playfully into his eyes.

Harrison looked straight at me. Were his eyes brown? Or were they almost green?

Suddenly, my mouth went dry. Any thought I had about yelling teachers versus apathetic teachers evaporated and was replaced by two extremely loud thoughts.

HARRISON IS CLOSE BY! yelled one part of my brain. *Don't do anything stupid!* advised the other half. I tried desperately not to stare at Harrison but I also tried not to look as though I were turning away from him. Our arms were practically touching.

What was the question? Something about teachers? "I really like Ms. Phelps," I finally managed to mumble. *Did I really just say that?*

The group groaned and the bell rang, signaling the end of lunch. Lauren rolled her eyes at me. "Um, *hello*, Lucy? Ms. Phelps wasn't one of the choices."

Ms. Phelps wasn't a yeller, but she wasn't a pushover, either. A lot of teachers spend the first week going over stuff we learned the year before, but Ms. Phelps plunged into new things right away. We were only supposed to have an hour of homework a night, but between strange word problems about painting houses with people named Mary and Steve, and having to write an essay about our three favorite books, I was lucky if I was done in three hours.

By Friday, I just wanted to go home and relax in my room one more time before Yi Po arrived. But when I got home from school, Mom was home early from work so that she could clean the house. As if Yi Po were traveling thousands of miles to see how clean our house was.

"Oh, good," she said as soon as I walked through the door. She was on her hands and knees, washing the tile floor in the family room. "You can help."

No *How was your day?* or *Would you like to help?* Hadn't she realized what a rough week it had been? I took off my backpack and let it drop to the floor, near where we kept our shoes.

"Lucy!" Mom barked. "I just washed the floor! Pick up that backpack!"

"It's not like my backpack is covered in dirt or something," I argued. "I'll pick it up in a minute."

"Now," Mom said in her do-it-or-else voice. "I don't need you undoing what I've already done when there are a million things to do before Yi Po arrives."

Something inside of me snapped. Mom was so concerned about making a good first impression that she had forgotten about me. *I* was the one who had to share her bedroom with a stranger. *I* was the one who was looking at the very real possibility of Saturday at Chinese school instead of basketball. *Would you rather go to Chinese school or play basketball?* Yeah, like it was even close.

"You want me to get ready for Yi Po? Fine." I ran up to my room and slammed the door shut.

I looked around the room. Madison and I had arranged it to maximize open space in the room by making an L-shape with the beds in one corner, and a study nook with a desk and bookcase in the other.

I'll get ready for Yi Po! I dragged the beds away from the corner and put them on opposite sides of the room. *There!* Then I pulled my desk to the middle of the room so that it stood between the two beds. For good measure, I dragged the bookcase until it was lined up next to the desk.

Now the desk and bookcase formed a wall between the two beds. *The Great Wall of Lucy Wu.* When I lay down on my bed, all I could see was my side of the desk and the front of the bookcase. And I hid my favorite picture of my grandmother, the last one we took before she got sick, in my bookcase.

"Lucy? What's all that racket? What is going on up here?" Mom pushed the door open. The beautiful room that Madison and I had made was gone. She turned and left. Kenny poked his head in, but didn't say anything.

You want ready? I'm ready. I was still breathing heavily from pulling all the furniture around. I folded my arms and lay in bed, waiting for a feeling of satisfaction to come, but it never did.

CHAPTER EIGHT

MOM, KENNY, AND I WENT TO THE AIRPORT THE NEXT day. While Dad's trips make me nervous, I like watching other people coming and going. You can feel this buzz of energy—people getting ready to travel to some exotic place, or just arriving home. There are the business travelers in their slick suits and people who look like they might have their own private jets. I like the grungy college types—the boys have ponytails or goatees and the girls have braids and cool-looking jewelry—who carry everything they have in tall, complicated-looking backpacks.

But I was not in a good mood. All I noticed today was the slight aroma of sweaty people everywhere and the fact that everything in the airport was incredibly expensive. My small Coke was three dollars! And we had been waiting for two hours already. The plane had finally arrived, but Mom said Dad and Yi Po were probably stuck in customs.

Kenny, Mom, and I sat in a row of beige plastic seats. I kept thinking that if we sat there much longer, our butts would take the shape of the chairs. Mom polished off a cup of coffee and I finished a bag of trail mix. Kenny had a fruit smoothie and a banana nut muffin in the first hour we were there, and then announced he needed an eight-inch meatball sub.

Kenny tilted his head toward the bank of monitors listing arriving and departing flights. "Have you noticed that most of the trips going east and north are even numbers, and the trips going west and south are odd numbers?"

"You are such a weirdo, Kenny," I told him, which he appeared to take as a compliment. I mean, he can't find his backpack when it's right in front of him, but he notices *this*?

I was so bored I was actually reading articles in the business section of the newspaper someone had left in the seat next to me. One article was about some business that specialized in finding Chinese-speaking nannies for parents in New York. Maybe *those* kids would like to go to Chinese school.

Then Mom jumped up. "They're here! Steve, over here!"

I saw Dad first, coming out of a long tunnel. He was walking more slowly than he usually did, and he was pulling a suitcase behind him. And then I saw *her*.

So this was going to be my roommate for the next three months. Her hair looked like short gray wire and her entire outfit was made of navy blue padded cotton. She looked like a tumbling mat with hair. When she saw us, she smiled, and I could see that she was missing a tooth.

This was my grandmother's sister? My grandmother had long soft hair, which she had let me brush for hours when I was little. She always wore something—a necklace or a scarf—that made her look special. And her smile was beautiful.

My mom hurried up to meet them and let loose a stream of welcoming Chinese. *Hello! Welcome! How was your trip? Have you eaten?*

Yi Po put up a hand and nodded. Mom dragged her over to meet Kenny and me.

"Ni hao," said Kenny. He put out his hand and they shook hands. Yi Po looked at Kenny and nodded approvingly. *"Ta hen gao!"* she said to Dad. *He's so tall!* Dad smiled and nodded.

Now it was my turn. My plan was to do exactly what Kenny did. I stuck out a hand and said, *"Ni hao."*

Yi Po looked at me and said, *"Ni hao."* Then she turned to my Dad again and this time she said, in Chinese:

SHE'S SO FAT!

Okay, technically, she didn't scream. It only *felt* that way. She also didn't say *fat* exactly. She said *da*, which means *big*. But for a person of limited verticality, *big* can really only mean one thing: You are big in the horizontal sense. It certainly *felt* like she was calling me fat.

I'm not fat. I'm not super skinny like Serena. I'm normal.

I turned around and started marching toward the parking lot. I would have given anything to have my grandmother here instead of *her*.

Mom grabbed my arm. "Why are you walking so far ahead of us? We're in no hurry. Show some manners."

"Manners?" I hissed through my teeth. "Did you *hear* what she said to me? You're talking to me about *manners*?"

Mom shook her head. "You two have barely spoken. What could she have said?"

I glared at Mom. "She said, *ta hen da*. She's *soooo* big."

Mom stopped walking and started laughing. "Lucy—don't be silly. She didn't mean that you were fat. She meant that you were older than she expected. You know, in English, like when you say someone's a big kid."

Oh. I stopped marching.

Mom walked back and repeated the story in Chinese to Yi Po, Dad, and Kenny, and they had a jolly good time laughing at my expense. Then, to make things worse, Dad pulled out Matilda in front of everyone in the parking lot to explain that Yi Po thought I was younger because I had given him a stuffed animal.

I hated them all right then and there, enough to drill a hole in a ground. I hated them for embarrassing me and laughing at me. But I also hated Yi Po for who she wasn't—she wasn't my grandmother, who had always known how old I was, and had given Matilda to me.

WHEN WE CAME HOME, MOM AND DAD SHOWED YI PO around the house. Then Mom told me it was my job to give Yi Po a tour of the bedroom. Our bedroom.

I opened the door to our room and hoped that the wall in the middle would explain everything. My side of the room was on the same side as the door; my bed was against the wall to the right, my dresser was behind the door, and the closet was at the end of the room. *Her* side also had a dresser, plus a bed under the window with a nightstand.

Kenny had brought up her suitcase and left it on her bed, in case there was any question of whose side was whose. Maybe she would figure out the whole deal, unpack her stuff quietly, and stay on her side of the room for the rest of her visit.

No such luck.

As soon as we walked into the room, she decided to take a tour of my side. *"Wah!"* she said. She pointed to my large collection of stuffed animals. Then she ran her fingers over the books in my bookcase.

How did you say *Don't touch my stuff* in Chinese? I walked over and slid the door open to her side of the closet, hoping that would bring her over to her side of the room. I smiled tightly, and waved my arm like a game show hostess. *Look! You've won half a closet!*

She didn't see me. She looked at the log cabin diorama I had made two years ago and picked up a picture of Madison and me in goggles and hats. We had been skiing. Did they have skiing in China?

I walked over and tapped Madison's face in the photo. *Peng you.* At least I knew that much. Friend.

I walked back to her side of the room now, hoping to lure her over to her side with a demonstration of the dresser and nightstand. She didn't follow me.

Now she was looking at my trophies, my basketball trophies from four seasons of league play plus two years of making it into the play-offs. She reached out and gently touched my favorite one, the one with a player in the middle of a hook shot.

She pointed to the trophies and asked a question. Uh-oh. I smiled politely and stood on her side of the room, waiting. This did not satisfy her. She pointed again and asked, but the sounds slipped by me again. I felt my heart speed up. *What was she saying?* I thought of the one question that everyone asked me, You *play basketball?* and decided to go with that. I pointed to the trophy and pointed to me. *Yes, those are mine.*

Yi Po sighed and shook her head, disappointed. That wasn't it, and a hot flush of embarrassment crept up my neck. She probably thought I was an idiot.

She walked slowly to her side of the room, and looked on as I pointed out her closet and dresser. Then, without another word, she started to unpack.

"So, how *did* you find Yi Po?" Kenny asked that night at dinner. Mom had made one of my dad's favorites, *shi zi tou,* or lion's head. When I was little, Kenny used to tease me that the baseball-sized meatballs were actually made from real lions, instead of ground pork.

Dad repeated the question to Yi Po in Chinese, and his face broke into a huge grin. It's the face he makes when he has a good story to tell.

"As you may be aware, I had been conducting my search for the world's most perfect bowl of noodles for some time now," he announced. "The search had reached worldwide proportions."

Kenny, Mom, and I gave a soft, collective sigh. Dad wasn't looking for just any bowl of noodles. He was looking for noodles like the ones Po Po used to make. My dad used to joke that he acted like the perfect son-in-law so Po Po would make him noodles, but the truth was they had just really adored each other. Dad repeated his announcement to Yi Po in Chinese, and she giggled.

Dad continued. "It became a running gag at the office. When will Steve find the perfect bowl of noodles? Then one day, Josie walks in and says that her cabbie told her about a noodle place that we have to go to. So at lunchtime, a bunch of us jumped into a cab and set off to find the place."

I picked up the serving spoon and helped myself to another lion's head and some of the cabbage.

"We finally get there, and it's this hole-in-the-wall type place featuring all kinds of noodles. There's a line out the door, and Sam's getting nervous because he's got a ton of work back at the office. We decide to stay, though, because everyone's talking about how good the noodles are and it smells *incredible*. We can even see the guys making different kinds of noodles—one of them is slicing noodles off a big block, another guy is pulling them. There's another guy who just shouts out the orders. We stood in line for fifteen or twenty minutes, and finally, we got our noodles."

After Dad translated, Yi Po nodded and moved her hands in a long stretching motion.

The way my dad used his hands and his voice, he made me feel like I was there with him. I could almost see the big pots of soup and the man in a greasy shirt yelling out orders as they come up. The restaurant was warm, almost hot, from cooking and the crowds of people who were talking, shouting, eating.

Dad paused. "I ask for a bowl that seems closest to Po Po's beef noodle soup. If you're looking for the world's most perfect noodles, after all, you have to have some sort of baseline for comparison. When the waiter delivers the bowl, it already looks very promising. The noodles are long, cut to the correct width. The broth smells lovely, and there are just a few green onions floating on the top.

"Is it too good to believe? After the first bite, I can't believe it. I want to weep. They are perfect. They are just like Po Po's. Perfect texture and the combination of beef and vegetables is just right." Dad leaned forward in his chair and we did, too, waiting for the bowl of noodles to appear.

I can't remember what Po Po's noodles tasted like anymore. I wish there were a way to record flavors the way you can record music, and then you could play it over and over in your mouth.

When Yi Po hears Dad's description of her noodles repeated in Chinese, she waves a hand modestly and shakes her head. "I finish my bowl and then get up and beg the guy to introduce me to the person who made the noodles. I have to know. I have to know what they did to make the noodles like Po Po's. At first he looks at me like I'm crazy. I know what he's thinking—it's flour, eggs, and water. The noodles are good, but how good can they be?

"I keep asking, though, and finally he relents, I think, just so I'll leave him alone. I figure it's one of these guys doing the noodle tricks at the front of the store, and I'll just wait until the right guy goes on break. But then, the guy I've been bugging walks out with Yi Po."

Dad shook his head. "For a minute, I thought I was hallucinating. Maybe I've been wanting Po Po's noodles for so long that now that I have them, my mind is making me think she's here again. But it's not her."

I couldn't believe Dad actually thought Yi Po and my grandmother looked anything alike. It wasn't even close. Then I had a thought—*Maybe she's an impostor! A con artist!* I started listening more closely for clues. Maybe my year wasn't ruined after all.

Yi Po added something to what Dad said, laughing the whole time. Mom translated: *My boss came into the kitchen. He said, Go out there and see what this guy wants. He's crazy!*

Yeah, right, I thought. *Your boss probably said, If you play your cards right, you can go to America with this businessman!*

Dad kept talking. "I couldn't say what I thought. Not right away. I don't want to scare her. And what if I'm wrong? So I start off, complimenting her on her noodles, how perfect they are. And she's nodding but waving off the compliments at the same time."

Kenny leaned forward. "What did you say next?"

"I'm thinking to myself, how can I get her to start thinking about this? It's a trick we use sometimes in negotiations—you drop little bread crumbs but let the other person think it's their idea. So I say, 'Your noodles remind me so much of my mother-in-law's. Maybe you're from the same place. She was from Shanghai.' Sure enough, her face lights up and she says, 'I'm from Shanghai, too!'"

Yi Po nodded and pointed from herself to me and Kenny. She said something in Chinese but all I could figure out was *Shanghai* and *noodle*. I wasn't fooled, though. *You would say you were from any province Dad asked about. You'd say you were from Mexico!*

Mom shook her head in disbelief. "Only you, Steve," she said.

"Now she's really interested in me. I'm not just some crazy guy anymore," Dad continued. "She says, 'What was your mother-in-law's surname? Maybe I knew her family.'" Dad puts up both hands, slowing down. "I turn to her and look her right in the face. I don't say anything for a moment so I know she's really listening. Then I say, 'I think you knew her. Her name was Bao Lihua.'"

Dad and Yi Po glance at each other. "She sat down and wiped her face," said Dad. "Then all she said was, 'Yes, I knew her.' And she looked at me, and we both knew what that meant." Yi Po looked at us and smiled.

No one said anything but I was practically bursting. *That's it! Dad gave her Po Po's name! He asked her if she was from Shanghai! She's never proven she's Po Po's sister! She could be anyone!* I felt like one of those lawyers on TV, ready to make the witness break down on the stand.

Before I could open my mouth, Dad started in again. "I started visiting Yi Po every day, eating her noodles and just letting us get to know each other. And then one day, I asked, 'Why don't you come with me to meet your family?' And do you know what she said?"

I narrowed my eyes at Yi Po. She might fool Mom and Dad, but she wasn't fooling me. *Yeah, I know what she said. Yippee! This sucker's finally invited me to America!*

"What did she say?" asked Mom.

"Of course, the first couple of times she said, 'No, it's too much trouble . . .'"

You got that right.

". . . but after a few more times she agreed. She said, 'Well, who wants to be a frog in a well?'" said Dad.

Yi Po nodded and added, *"Jing di zhi wa,"* as if we hadn't heard that phrase a million times before.

My accusations melted away. Po Po's favorite phrase. I looked at her hands, tapping the kitchen table. Perfect oval fingernails, just like my grandmother's. I couldn't deny it. This was her sister, and her noodles had ruined my life.

CHAPTER NINE

WITHIN A FEW DAYS OF YI PO'S ARRIVAL, I REALIZED that I should have built a much bigger wall, instead of just the desk-bookshelf wall down the middle of the room. I was in the middle of an all-out assault on the senses. Even if I walked around my room with my eyes closed, I could still smell her and hear her. There was no escape.

My room—or should I say, our room—now smelled like the main factory for Vicks VapoRub. Yi Po really seemed to love the mentholated stuff, even though she wasn't sick, and I was fairly sure that I would not be having any respiratory problems just from the secondary fumes. I told Madison that I wanted to hang a huge plastic shower curtain down the middle of the room to protect me from the smell, until Madison pointed out that the smell of a new plastic shower curtain is not a huge improvement over Vicks. And, anyway, a plastic shower curtain wouldn't protect me from . . .

WCHI—your station for Chinese news, music, sports, and weather! Okay, I didn't actually know whether that was what the radio announcers were saying, but I did know that within twenty-four hours of arriving, Yi Po had managed to find a radio station that provided all-Chinese programming throughout the day. Who knew? We had lived here for years without knowing about the station. Although reception wasn't perfect, Yi Po seemed perfectly happy to listen to whatever staticky news that station served up. *Crrrrkkkk! Ssscccccrrrtttccch! Zwakkkk!* The noise drove me crazy.

For *that* I thought about having a five-inch-thick steel wall. Sure, it might be a little awkward, unattractive, and expensive, but it might deflect the radio waves, and also block the smells and the other sounds that came from across the room. And by "other sounds," I mean the ones that started at *five o'clock* in the morning.

Yes, Yi Po woke up every day before the sun even peeped out. And did she tiptoe out quietly? Not without making the bed! I lay in bed and listened to her every morning, walking around in her flat slippers that made a *fwap-fwap* sound with every step. I soon noticed that she had a little pattern every morning. *Whoosh fwap-fwap.* She pulled up the blankets. *Swish fwap-fwap.* She smoothed the bed. *Poom fwap-fwap.* She puffed up the pillow.

By the time she *fwap-fwapp*ed out of the room, I was too *fwapp*ing mad to go back to sleep.

I tried complaining to Mom, to see if Mom could get her to stop. Mom wouldn't help me. "Old people are pretty set in their ways," she informed me. "I doubt she can help it. Why don't you try going to bed earlier?"

"How much earlier?" I asked her. "When I get home from school?"

The truth of the matter was, when I really thought about it, there probably wasn't a wall wide enough, tall enough, or thick enough to keep me from forgetting Yi Po was here for a long, long time.

ONE NIGHT I GRUMBLED TO KENNY AS HE READ A FAT book on World War II. "You're so lucky you don't have to share a room with her," I said. "It stinks in there and she's up at the crack of dawn. I hate it."

"It could be a lot worse, Lucy. She's been through a lot, you know," Kenny said, half-reading his book.

I sighed. "Yeah, I know. Her mom, dad, and sister went to the U.S. and never came back for her." I held up my hand and made the *blah blah blah* motion.

"No, not that," Kenny sat up. "I mean, yeah, that's a lot, but she's been through much more than that. War, of course, and famine. And you know about the Cultural Revolution in the sixties, right?"

I had heard the words *Cultural Revolution* before, but I thought it was about music and painting.

Kenny shook his head. "Mao Zedong, China's leader, said that China needed to let go of their old ways, have a huge revolution. And some students, called Red Guards, took it to the extreme."

"Extreme? Like . . ."

"Mao also told people to get rid of their Four Olds— old ideas, customs, habits, and culture. The Red Guards used this idea as a reason to go after people, tear apart their homes, making sure they didn't have any Four Olds objects, or anything Western. Sometimes kids even informed on their own parents to prove their loyalty to Mao. I mean, we're used to Regina ratting us out to Mom and Dad, but what if Regina reported on Mom and Dad, or one of her teachers? That's what it was like."

I pulled my knees up against me.

Kenny went on. "And the crimes people committed, they weren't *crime* crimes. Not like robbery or murder. They were crimes like teaching Shakespeare, or having a father who had been a landlord."

"That's not fair," I objected. "You can't control what your parents did."

"It happened anyway, Lucy. And many people didn't even do what they had been accused of, though the Red Guards tried to force them to confess by beating and humiliating them. There were a lot of suicides."

"So what are you saying? I should sleep with the lights on?" I didn't want to talk about the Cultural Revolution or Yi Po anymore.

Kenny leaned over. "I'm saying, she probably saw some pretty horrible things. Take it easy on her, okay?"

I didn't say anything.

"Okay?" Kenny repeated.

"Maybe," I said.

There was only one way I could think of to take it easy on Yi Po. I started staying outside for as long as possible. I either stayed at Madison's house, or if Madison wasn't home, I hung out in the driveway, practicing. Ten layups, ten three-pointers from the right, and then ten from the left. I even did fifty free throws a night, like Coach Mike wanted me to. As the days went by, more and more of my shots started going in, especially the free throws. *If Yi Po doesn't leave soon*, I thought, *I might make the Olympics.*

I saw her watching me from the window once. After that, I had a special dribble, just for her:

Go home! Go home! Go home!

CHAPTER TEN

MADISON AND I HAVE THIS JOKE THAT EVERYBODY HAS secret powers. The problem is, the powers are not all that powerful and they're *really* secret, so secret that you might not know you have them. Madison's secret power is that she always knows exactly which pair of shoes to wear. My secret power is that I can sharpen a pencil perfectly *the first time*, without the lead breaking.

My dad's secret power is that his hair always looks perfect, even after a long day at work. We like to say that Dad has Anchorman Hair. Now, even though Dad was at the office all day, every hair was positioned exactly where it should be. This is what I was thinking when Dad said he wanted to have a talk with me about Chinese school.

When your parents say they want to have a talk, what they really mean is you need to have a listen. I had been hoping that maybe my parents would just forget about Chinese school in the excitement over Yi Po. No such luck. I decided to take a different approach.

"Qing zuo, qing zuo." I said, patting the chair next to me. I wanted to remind him that I could speak *some* Chinese after the disaster at the airport.

Dad pretended to wobble as he high-stepped over a pile of laundry. *"Ni bie na me ke qi,"* he teased back. *Don't be so polite!*

Maybe this was going to be easier than I thought.

Dad grabbed the chair and flipped it around so he could rest his arms on the back. "So, your mother tells me that you don't want to go to Chinese school, that you don't want any extra school," he said.

I laid out my case. "Well, yeah. Not to mention the fact that I'd have to give up basketball. I feel like I've already given up a lot because Yi Po is staying in my room, and giving up basketball to go to some boring old Chinese school on top of that is just not fair."

"I think you are overlooking the long-term advantages of the situation here, Lucy." Sometimes I think my dad goes on business trips for so long he forgets how to talk like a normal person. "This is an opportunity to improve your Chinese. China is becoming a very important country in our future, and knowing Chinese may help you get a great job."

"I can already speak Chinese, a little, and any job that doesn't involve basketball isn't a great job to me," I pointed out.

"Well, that's another thing. What kind of future do you really think you have in basketball? I mean, *really*. You're getting older now, Lucy. You need to start thinking about how you spend your time, and what activities are going to pay off for you in high school, college, or even beyond that."

My parents have never been enthusiastic about my basketball the way they have about Regina's Chinese club or even Kenny's supposed math abilities. Still, they showed up for my games and Dad put up a basketball hoop in the driveway so that I could practice. Now it all felt like a big lie.

"What are you saying? That basketball is a waste of my time?" I tried to sound tough and businesslike, the way Dad did, but inside I was shaking.

"If you could do both, fine," Dad responded. "But we

must make a choice now, and Chinese school is the smart choice. Can you name any Chinese-Americans making a living in basketball?" He added quickly, "Who aren't over seven feet tall?"

I couldn't think of anyone. "I could be the first."

Dad shook his head. "I'm not saying this to be mean. I'm saying this because I want you to have as many options in the future as possible. Basketball doesn't provide many options for you—as an adult, I can see that. Speaking Chinese brings many options. And now is the best time for you to work on your Chinese."

"Basketball is really good exercise." It was a desperation play. The long heave-ho down the court at the buzzer. Even as I said that, a good kid argument to a parent, I hated myself for saying it. I didn't play basketball for *exercise*.

"If you're worried about exercise, you can take up tennis, if you like. Mom says there's talk of organizing some tennis classes on the courts after Chinese school." Dad stood up and brushed his hands together, as if he had finished a job. *Lucy goes to Chinese school*, check.

Next item. The words rolled out smoothly and lightly, as if Dad had been waiting to make that argument. I suddenly pictured Dad and Mom sitting together, plotting. *Let's cover every case for going to Chinese school and giving up that stupid, waste-of-time basketball.* A hot river of lava began to burn in my chest.

"Tennis is stupid," I said. "And Chinese school is even more stupid."

Dad acted like he hadn't heard me. "By the way, Mom said that we're going to have snacks tonight and just have a chance to sit down with Yi Po. It would be a great chance for you to practice your Chinese. You can listen and ask questions. You could even learn some Shanghainese if you want."

"I can practice my Chinese with Yi Po? I can learn Shanghainese? Gee, *thanks*," I said sarcastically. "What makes you think you can make me speak *one more word* to her?" Even though the words flew out faster than my brain could process them, at that moment I meant it.

Dad threw up his hands. My dad has a long fuse, but when he gets mad, he's really mad. "This discussion is over," he thundered, his face turning red. "All I know is that you *will* be at Chinese school next week. Ten o'clock sharp!" Dad walked out of the room.

"And I'll hate every minute of it!" I screamed back at him. And I was going to make them hate it, too, if I could. Enough to force them to stop making me go.

EVEN THOUGH DAD AND I HAD BEEN YELLING AT EACH other a few hours earlier, Dad acted like nothing was wrong when it was time for what he called "our family get-together." Like we were some old-fashioned family on TV, gathering around the fireplace to make yarn or something.

"C'mon, Lucy. We'll have snacks in the family room," said Dad.

I glared at him, but only until I saw Mom walk by with a tray full of Chinese goodies, including one of my favorites, *chen pi mei*, candied plums. But I wasn't going to be bought off that easily.

"I have a project for school," I told him, pulling out the trump card: school.

Dad nodded, approving of my wise decision. "Maybe next week."

What I didn't say was that my project for school was getting even for having to go to Chinese school. If Chinese school was going to ruin my life, it was going to ruin *everybody's* life. I wrote out a plan.

1. Ignore parents if they speak in Chinese. Force them to yell in English.
2. Ask for non-Chinese food when we go out to Chinese restaurants. The more American, the better. *While they're having the* ma po tofu, *may I have a hamburger and French fries? Make mine medium well.*
3. Complain about going to Chinese school while going there.
4. Complain about what happened in Chinese school on the way home.
5. If forced, absolutely forced, to speak Chinese, insist on having really weird words translated. What's the Chinese word for *ambidextrous*?

homogenized? *platypus*? Possible sentence: *I put my homogenized milk next to the ambidextrous platypus.*

Chinese school itself was a little trickier. I wasn't sure I could go for all-out bad student, like Jamie Watkins who was always talking back to Ms. Phelps, or Paul Terry over in Mrs. Tibbs's class, who was already famous for asking questions that eventually made the teacher contradict herself. Since I really wanted to minimize my talking time in Chinese school, neither of these boys seemed like a decent role model. I was starting to feel desperate, when I remembered someone else: Amelia Helprin.

Amelia drifted into our class last year around Thanksgiving and stayed until spring break. She had white-blond hair and eyes so pale blue I had a hard time looking her in the eye. As far as I could tell, Amelia basically said two things: "I don't know" and "I don't want to." Her voice was light and feathery, and she spoke with no emotion or expression.

Amelia, would you like to read the next paragraph? *I don't want to.*

Amelia, would you please explain reducing fractions? *I don't know how.*

It was like trying to make a puddle of milk stand up. And the beauty of it all was that Ms. Pendergast usually ended up getting mad and tense, and Amelia stayed calm and cool.

I could do that. I could pull an Amelia. All I had to do now was wait until Chinese school started.

CHAPTER ELEVEN

WHEN I TOLD MADISON ABOUT DAD FORCING ME TO GO
to Chinese school, she groaned.

"What? You're going to miss the whole season?" Her
voice squeaked over the phone.

"Yeah, can you believe it? For *Chinese* school. Ugh."

Madison made some more appropriately sympathetic
sounds. Then she said, "But . . ."

"But what? There is no *but* in this situation."

"I dunno. I mean, I'm totally bummed about basketball, but it *is* kind of cool that you'll learn to speak
Chinese."

"I speak Chinese! Well, some, anyway. Listen to this,
I made this up this morning as part of my anti-Chinese
school campaign." I held the phone slightly away from
my mouth as I sang.

Yi, er, san, si, wu, liu, qi
Who likes Chinese school?

Not me!
Not for me! Not for me!
Chinese school is not for me!

"What is that, the part you sing in the beginning?" asked Madison.

"I'm counting. It's a song from my *Chinese Baby* video," I told her. I had already started singing it around the house. Yi Po was probably wondering if I would ever make it to eight.

"Wow," said Madison.

"Pretty good, huh?" I said proudly.

"Actually," said Madison, "your singing is really *bad*."

I TRIED NOT TO ACT TOO BUMMED OUT ABOUT BASKET-ball around Madison—I didn't want to make her feel bad for playing. Madison tried not to talk too much about basketball around me—even though I did catch her diagramming a play on the back of her math home-work. "Sorry," she said, crumpling up the paper. She looked guilty.

"Don't be," I said. But it made me feel sad. Who was she going to run the play with? Bethany? Kelly? I guess it didn't matter. The answer was: Not Me.

IF THAT WASN'T BAD ENOUGH, I CROSSED THE WALL.

I had been making it a point for me, and my stuff, not to cross over to Yi Po's side of the room. I did this even though I was slowly discovering that the smaller space seemed to make everything squeeze and pop out of drawers and fall off the shelves. I did this even though Yi Po seemed to have plenty of space, and her side was always clean. The wall had a purpose, and so far, I had stayed on my side, and Yi Po had stayed on hers.

This morning, though, I had an emergency.

It started when I woke up and realized the clock said 7:47, which is bad, because I usually wake up at 7:05. The alarm hadn't gone off! I had thirteen minutes to get dressed, find colored pencils for my South American map project, eat breakfast, and get to school on time. I hate being late—I feel like I'm never caught up for the rest of the day.

Part of the problem was my dresser was on the opposite side of the room from my closet. It was the only place it would go with the wall in the middle of the room. So while my T-shirts, underwear, and socks were on one side of the room in the dresser, my jeans, hoodies, and shoes were on the other side in the closet. Going back and forth between these two places is not exactly easy, since I have to squeeze through the small space between my bed and my desk. My half of the room had become a small landfill with clothes, shoes, books, and an occasional basketball.

So getting dressed went something like this: pick out shirt, *hop hop* to other side of room, find jeans, *hop trip*, go back for socks. I was about to get dressed when Yi Po walked in.

Hop hop DIVE. I threw myself under the covers of the bed. I felt kind of weird about getting dressed in front of her.

"Lucy!" Mom yelled from downstairs. "Shouldn't you be leaving for school?"

I stuck my head out from under the covers. "I'm almost ready!"

Yi Po wandered back out of the bedroom, and I jumped out of bed and finished getting dressed. Well, okay, I jumped out of bed, got dressed, and almost sprained my ankle on the pile of math worksheets I'd left on the floor.

As I bent down to rub my ankle, I spotted the colored pencils I needed under my desk. I reached under the desk and grabbed the box, being careful not to bang my head as I stood up.

Unfortunately, I was *not* careful to pick up the box from the right side, and twelve pencils slid out onto the floor, rolling away from me onto Yi Po's side. *Grrrr*. I decided that just this once, I would cross over to Yi Po's side to pick up the pencils, and then cut through her side to leave, saving time by not going back through the Lucy Obstacle Course.

I had taken about three steps through her side when,

like a police car cutting off a fugitive running down an alleyway, Yi Po appeared, cutting off my access to the door. *Busted.*

I stared at her. What was she going to say? *What are you doing, running through my half of the room?*

"*Mei Mei,*" said Yi Po. She pointed to the window, and then pretended to shiver. "*Tian qi hen leng.*" *It's cold.*

I looked out the window and saw the trees moving slightly. It didn't look that cold. I calculated how long it would take to convince her I would not be cold, versus just getting a sweatshirt. I ran back to my closet, grabbed a sweatshirt, and ran back across the room, this time on *my* side.

Now she was in the doorway.

Arrrgh. I bounced impatiently behind her, trying not to scream.

This only made her turn around in the doorway.

Yi Po reached out and patted my sweatshirt. "*Hen ke ai!*" she said. *Cute.* Then she moved around me to go back into the bedroom. Slowly.

Argh! Why was she standing in the doorway if she wasn't leaving? I was about to run down the stairs when I happened to catch a glance back toward the bedroom.

She was cleaning up my clothes. Picking them up, shaking them out, folding them.

"No!" I dropped my backpack and sweatshirt, and went back in. Now that I had been on her side of the room, Yi Po seemed to think she was allowed on my side. Plus if Mom caught her cleaning my side of the room I would be deader than dead meat. Not that I could explain all that, so instead, I said, *"Bu hao yi si."*

The words felt funny and dry in my mouth, even though it was a phrase I'd heard about a thousand times. *Bu hao yi si* covered a lot of ground between *I'm sorry* and *I'm embarrassed* and a polite version of *You shouldn't have done that*, which was exactly what I needed. The literal translation was *not good meaning*, which I meant, too.

"Mei guanxi," replied Yi Po. *It's fine.* She picked up a pair of jeans and folded them in half.

I tugged on the jeans, trying to get her to let go of them. *"Bu hao yi si,"* I repeated.

With my Chinese vocabulary used up for the morning, I made wide circling motions with my arms to indicate my half of the room. Then I patted my chest. I hoped my meaning was clear: *I'll do it myself.*

"Lucy, what's going on here? You should have left for school by now." Mom walked in and saw Yi Po holding my jeans. She put her hands on her hips. "Lucy Mengxue Wu! Is Yi Po cleaning your room?"

"No, I . . ." But Mom wouldn't let me explain.

"This is terrible! Yi Po shouldn't be cleaning your room. You need to clean up your room!" Then she turned to Yi Po and starting apologizing. I heard her say, *"Bu hao yi si."*

Hadn't I just said that? Wasn't I trying to get Yi Po to stop cleaning my room?

I grabbed my stuff and headed down the stairs. It was so unfair—even when I tried to do the right thing, I managed to get in trouble when Yi Po was around.

● ● ●

I SLID INTO MY SEAT WITH ABOUT A MINUTE TO spare. Ms. Phelps had an announcement.

"I understand that there's a rumor that we might have a sixth-grade dance this year." Madison and I looked at each other, eyebrows raised. The school usually had some kind of community fund-raiser by the sixth grade, and a school dance had been mentioned as a possibility. I hadn't even decided how I felt about a dance.

"We may have a dance at the end of the year, but for now, we've decided to do something a little different to benefit our community," she went on. "The week before Thanksgiving, we're going to have a sixth grade versus faculty basketball game. Admission to the game will be a can of food, which will be donated to a food pantry."

Did she just say basketball?! I held my hand under the desk for a high five. Madison reached over and tickled my palm. *We were still going to play together!* This was way better than a dance. And those teachers didn't know what they were in for.

Ms. Phelps grinned. "*And* to make things even more interesting, we're going to have a contest to see who will be the captain of the sixth graders. The winner will be chosen according to how many free throws you can make in a row."

Oscar said, "Then the captain will be Paul Terry." Some other boys groaned in agreement. Paul Terry was a total show-off on the court, hogging the ball and screaming when he made a basket. Paul was tall enough now that he was getting close to dunking. There was a rumor that his dad had played for the Boston Celtics for a while, but I had never seen his dad. I had only seen his mom, who always looked a little worn out, possibly from having a kid like Paul.

Madison pointed at me and mouthed *you*. When I looked around, Serena, Haley, and Lauren were turned around in their seats, nodding.

I pointed back at Madison. "You should try out for captain, too," I whispered.

Madison shook her head. "No way." She turned to the others and jerked her thumb at me. "She's been practicing like crazy. Fifty free throws a day." I couldn't help grinning. Even if my parents wouldn't let me go to basketball practice, they couldn't stop me from playing basketball for school. It was practically homework! And I had noticed something about Paul Terry that Oscar and the other boys had not figured out. For all his showing off on the court and fancy moves, Paul stinks at free throws.

This is it, I thought. *I'm finally going to have the year I've been waiting for.* I could see sixth graders gathered around me, with the score tied and seconds to go, and I call the critical play to win the game. My parents would meet me after the game and say, "Honey, we made a terrible mistake making you go to Chinese school instead of basketball practice." Maybe even Harrison would say something.

It all seemed perfect until Serena told me about Sloane Connors at lunch.

Sloane Connors is in the other sixth grade class, Mrs. Tibbs's class. Some people think she's pretty, including Sloane, I'm sure, but to me, she always looks like she's sneering, even when she smiles. Adults like Sloane because she volunteers to help and has good manners, at least around them. At school, though, the kids know not to cross Sloane. She's the head of a little group that Madison and I secretly call the Amazons, and they can make your life miserable in about a thousand different ways. They'll even go after one of their own. Two years ago, an Amazon named Kendra threw a birthday party at a hotel pool. Sloane wasn't able to go because her family went out of town that weekend. Sloane thought Kendra had chosen that date on purpose, and suddenly, Kendra wasn't invited to any more birthday parties and was sitting alone at lunch. Rumors started popping up everywhere: *Kendra has head lice. Kendra was caught shoplifting.* The next year, Kendra switched to a private school.

"Guess who's going to go for captain in Mrs. Tibbs's class?" Serena bit into her tuna fish sandwich. "Sloane Connors."

I dropped my apple and groaned. I did not want to be in a competition against Sloane. Madison turned toward Serena and said, "I didn't even know that Sloane played basketball."

"She doesn't," said Serena. "I bet she just likes the

idea of getting to boss everyone around. You know how she loves being the center of attention."

I closed my eyes and put my head down on the table, feeling the cool smooth surface against my forehead. *Think.* From this position, I could smell mustard and the slightly pasty smell of noodles. I could also see Talent, sitting by herself. She was reading a book while she ate a sandwich.

"Are you okay?" asked Madison.

"Yeah, I'm fine," I said, taking a deep breath and sitting back up. "Okay, here's the plan. *Nobody* should say *anything* about me trying out for captain. Let's just keep this our little secret."

Madison and Haley nodded in agreement. Serena, however, looked sheepish.

"Oh," she said. "I wish you'd said something sooner."

Sloane didn't wait long. She found me after school the next day while I waited for Madison to go back for her jacket.

"Hey, Lucy," she said, all fake-friendly. "I heard you're going out for captain of the basketball team."

"I might," I said. The less I said, the better.

"You do want the sixth grade to win, don't you?" Sloane asked, looking serious.

"Sure." Where was she going with this?

Sloane licked her lips and moved in for the kill. "I do, too. I just don't want the team to come up . . . *short.*" She took a step toward me, forcing me to tilt my neck back to look at her. Did I mention that Sloane is extremely tall?

"I don't think we have to worry about Lucy coming up with anything but a win," a voice said behind me. I hadn't heard Madison come up.

Sloane acted as if she hadn't heard Madison. "Listen, Lucy, if this were for something like, I don't know, *math* team, you'd get my vote in a heartbeat. But think about it. If you make captain, and the team loses, everyone is going to blame you, 'cause who ever heard of a basketball team lead by some short Chinese girl?"

I rolled my eyes at her, but my heart felt like it had fallen into my stomach. First my dad and now Sloane.

Madison cut between me and Sloane. "That is a racist . . ."

"Don't call me a racist," Sloane said sharply. "I'm not saying *I* believe it, I'm just saying that's what other people think."

"I, for one, don't think that's true, and I'm sure most people would agree," said Madison. "And I don't think we have to worry about losing because Lucy actually plays basketball, unlike some people, and she's pretty good at it." Madison looked at Sloane pointedly.

"Yeah, I know," said Sloane dismissively. "Ms. Phelps got all the girl jock wannabes, didn't she? You guys and Serena, too. But really, who do you think the boys would *really* like to listen to?" She gave her thick hair a little toss, in case we had missed her point. "I really am thinking of what's best for the team. No offense."

"Let's just take it to the free-throw line, okay, Sloane? Lucy's already in training, putting in fifty free throws a day," retorted Madison. "I haven't seen you put up a decent free throw *ever*." This was Madison's loyal side coming out, though I really wanted to whisper, *Not right now!*

For the first time, Sloane's cool demeanor dropped. "Have you really? Been putting in fifty a day?" asked Sloane, her sleek eyebrows rising in surprise.

I nodded, trying to look as if I didn't care. Sloane turned to go. "Have it your way. I just thought that if we knew who the captain was early, it would be better for the team."

"Whatever, Sloane," I said to her back, although I didn't really want her to hear me.

Madison fumed all the way home. She basically said three things over and over. "She doesn't even play basketball!" "You've *totally* got to go out for captain now," and "Who do you think the boys will listen to?" When she said the last phrase, she swung her ponytail around dramatically, imitating Sloane.

"She's delusional," I said weakly.

"Yeah," said Madison. "You'll show her. You'll mop up the court with her. You're way better."

While I was pretty sure that I was better than Sloane

at basketball, I was even more sure that I didn't want to be Kendrafied.

We reached Madison's house. She reached up and opened the mailbox, took out the mail, and closed the door with a smooth click. "Want to come in?"

"Not today," I said. I wanted to be alone.

"See you, Lumpy Warrior," she said.

I froze. Did she say *warrior*? I felt more like a coward with each passing minute.

"See you, um, Mouse Jeans."

Madison wrinkled her nose. "Not your best one."

No kidding.

WHEN I GOT HOME, I RAN UPSTAIRS TO MY ROOM AND dove onto the bed.

BAM! My face thudded against the open jewelry box I had left near my pillow that morning, looking for the perfect pair of earrings. *Ow!* I wasn't sure what hurt more, the hard sides of the jewelry box or the prickly, pointy edges of the jewelry itself.

Stupid jewelry box. I picked it up and tossed it onto my

desk. The box bounced against a pile of books and fell to the floor, spilling necklaces and earrings on the way down.

My side of the room looked the way I felt. Jumbled, messy, slightly out of control.

I stood on my side of the wall and looked at Yi Po's side. It was orderly and tidy, but not in an overly fussy way. The covers of the bed were smooth and flat, like the ocean on a calm day. Her nightstand had two books, a clock, and a glass of water.

I wondered if she felt the way her side of the room looked: peaceful and simple. And I wondered what she thought of me on my side of the room.

THE FOLLOWING DAY WE HAD A SPELLING TEST. Ms. Phelps always scheduled spelling tests first thing in the morning, so I hurried to my seat to take one last look at the words.

WHAM! For a second, I didn't know what had happened, and then I realized that I was sitting on the floor. And my butt really hurt.

Ms. Phelps hurried over. "Are you okay, Lucy?"

"I think so." I got to my feet and looked down. One of the back legs of my chair was sticking straight out of the back.

Ms. Phelps picked up the chair and examined it. "I hope the other chairs don't malfunction." *Malfunction* was one of our spelling words.

"I'm sure it's just this one," I told her. But I was thinking of Sloane. *Bu hao yi si.*

Madison leaned over and whispered, "Are you okay? You didn't hurt your shooting hand, right?" She grinned at me. My stomach tightened and squeezed. Maybe that's exactly what Sloane had wanted to happen.

"Settle down," said Ms. Phelps. "Get out a clean sheet of paper and a pencil for your spelling test."

Or maybe it was just an accident. Accidents happen. *Please, please be an accident.*

"*Unnecessary,*" called Ms. Phelps. "A winter coat in the summer is *unnecessary.*"

I wrote the word down as my brain came up with another sentence.

Getting on Sloane's bad side was unnecessary.

CHAPTER TWELVE

FRIDAY WAS LIBRARY DAY. I TOSSED MY BOOK IN THE return slot and started looking over the Recent Arrivals display. I needed something new to read for my thirty minutes of reading every night. Madison headed over to the history section. Harrison — as much as I could tell without being obvious about it — was looking at *Sports Illustrated*. I wondered if he was going to go out for the basketball team.

Mrs. Anderson, who has been the librarian at Westgate since before Regina went to school, was just adding a book to the display. She has at least half a dozen pairs of glasses in different colors to coordinate with her outfits. Today she had on a pair of red glasses and a matching red jacket. "Looking for something particular?" she asked. I shook my head.

Mrs. Tibbs's class was also at the library. Sloane was holding court with the Amazons at a table near the windows. "Hi, Lucy," Sloane called over a little too loudly.

She tapped an empty chair at the next table. "Come and have a *seat.*" They all burst out laughing.

I had actually double-checked my seat that morning, putting my backpack on it first to see if it would fall down. *So it had been her.* I turned around and walked away so they couldn't see my expression.

"Girls," Mrs. Anderson called over to the Amazons. "Is there a problem?"

"Oh, no, Mrs. A.," said Sloane in a cheerful, good-girl voice. "We just wanted Lucy to sit with us." One of Sloane's friends, Nadia, let out a snort.

I don't know if there's a word for how I felt, unless there's a word for when you feel angry, embarrassed, and scared all at the same time. I grabbed the first book I saw and then looked around for Madison.

"It was *Sloane,*" I whispered. "She must have loosened the screws in my chair." Madison flipped open the book she was holding so we could pretend to be discussing it.

I was kind of hoping that Madison would say, *It was Sloane? That's scary. You better not try out for captain.* But

Madison made a deep growling noise. I recognized that sound. She usually made it after she'd been fouled.

"Well, she picked the wrong person to mess with. You are *so* going to devastate her in that free-throw contest."

Had Madison forgotten about Kendra? Sloane's penchant for search-and-destroy missions?

"It's over a whole month until the free-throw contest," I said, hoping that Madison would get my point, which was: A lot can happen in a month.

"Exactly," said Madison. "Enough time to completely perfect your technique so that you will humiliate Sloane."

In my mind, the words in Madison's sentence were slightly out of order. She should have said, *Sloane will humiliate you.*

"She knows how awesome you are," Madison went on. "That's what the problem is. She knows that you are going to be captain."

You know how a really good friend, a *great* friend, always thinks you're better than you actually are? Smarter, funnier, cuter, and just generally more amazing than you might realistically expect yourself to be? Madison had always been that friend for me, but I did not need that right now. I needed the friend that said, *You're a coward and that's okay.*

"Something could come up," I pointed out.

"Nope," said Madison. "It will be you. I just know it."

That's exactly what I was afraid of.

I DIDN'T THINK THE DAY COULD GET MUCH WORSE. BUT then it did, at lunch.

"Um, can I sit with you guys?" Talent stood next to our table, looking hopeful with a tray in her hands. "They need the table I normally sit at for the second-grade art show."

I looked at Madison, Serena, and Haley, and they looked back at me across the table. We had been involved in a discussion about boys and who liked who. I tried to send Madison a mental message: *Please, not today.*

"Of course," said Madison, not getting my message. She scooched her chair over so that Talent could sit between her and Haley. "Plenty of room." Even though Talent was the reason that I was missing basketball, Madison couldn't help being nice. It was genetic.

There was an awkward silence as Talent squeezed in. No one wanted to talk about boys anymore, not with Talent there.

"So, have you picked someone for your biography project?" Talent asked Madison. We had to write a biography of someone we admired.

"Not yet," said Madison. "You?"

Talent took a sip of milk and patted her mouth with a napkin. "I have it narrowed down to Madeleine Albright, the first female secretary of state, or Patsy Mink, the first Asian-American congresswoman." She took a sip of milk. "They're both so interesting. I'm having a hard time deciding. What about you, Serena?"

I wondered if Talent had a book at home: *Historical Women for Boring School Reports.*

Serena laughed. "Maybe I'll just take whoever you don't pick!" Serena liked doing her projects at the last minute.

"It has to be someone *you* admire," said Talent seriously. "Maybe you should pick an Olympic gymnast. Or a really successful coach."

Serena paused, thinking it over. "That's not a bad idea," she admitted.

"What about you?" Talent asked me.

"Pat Summitt," I said.

"I've never heard of Pat Summitt," said Talent. "Who is he?"

Madison covered her face. "Oh, man, you did not just say that."

"Here it comes," said Haley.

I glared at Talent. "*She* is the coach of the University of Tennessee Lady Volunteers basketball team. *She* is the winningest college basketball coach of all time among men and women's teams. *Pat Summitt* is the coach Madison and I plan to play for because *her* teams have been going to the national championships regularly for over thirty years," I said. *How could Talent not have heard of Pat Summitt?*

Talent ducked her head. "Oh, okay, Pat's a she. Got it. Sorry. She sounds, um, nice."

Madison patted Talent's arm. "Don't worry. When the Lady Vols win another championship with Lucy and me, you can say you knew us way back when. You can say you remember Lucy being captain of the sixth-grade basketball team."

"Wait—you've been picked as captain already?" Talent looked confused.

"No, no, no," I said. "Madison's just being nice." *Talent was so clueless sometimes!*

"Madison's just being truthful," said Madison. "Lucy's developing an unbeatable free throw, which is what you need to be captain. She's been practicing every day for weeks. No one is going to beat her."

"Who else is going out for captain?" asked Talent.

"Sloane Connors," said Madison. "And she doesn't even play basketball."

"Oh," said Talent. She turned to me. "Then you will be captain. You deserve it." In that split second, I almost liked Talent, just because in spite of everything, it was nice to get a vote of confidence. But then she had to go and ruin it.

"But you do know that Chinese school is more important, right?"

When we walked home from school, I was worried that Madison would bring up the free-throw contest again, but she was on to other things—we needed to plan our birthday party. After years of waiting, Halloween was going to be on a Saturday night—the perfect day to have a big bash. Madison's birthday is October 15, sixteen days before Halloween, and my birthday is November 16, sixteen days after. It was one of those amazing coincidences that made us best friends.

"Okay," said Madison, flopping onto her bed with a notebook. "It's going to be here, right?"

I kicked at the rug. "We're *supposed* to have it at my house. After three years of having it at your house . . ." I felt bad that Madison's family kept hosting our joint party. It had always been at Madison's house because Regina complained. "We can't possibly have it here," she'd whine to my parents. "I have to study." *Study* was the magic word, even though studying on a Saturday night was a stretch, even for Regina.

"It's really not a big deal, Lucy," said Madison.

"I'm going to ask, anyway," I said. "They should do *something*. I am their daughter, and they need to think of me, too."

Madison rolled her eyes. "Your aunt's not a piece of furniture, you know. You can't just shove her up in the attic when you don't want her around."

"Don't give me any ideas," I said. That morning Yi Po had tried to give me some mushy rice porridge for breakfast. It looked like white vomit.

Madison went over our party list.

"Type of cake?" asked Madison.

"Chocolate," I said.

"Check. Ice cream?"

"Strawberry and vanilla," I said. Madison and I both love chocolate cake and hate chocolate ice cream.

"Party schedule?"

"Early dinner, put on costumes, go trick-or-treating. Return for gifts and movies," I said with military crispness.

"Barcroft Oaks?"

Ah, the major question of the day. Barcroft Oaks was a twenty-minute walk away. On the other hand, it was a swanky neighborhood and lots of houses gave out full-size candy bars in Barcroft Oaks. Last year, someone had given out flashlights and soy energy drinks.

"Let's do it," I decided. We might not be trick-or-treating again.

"Movies?"

"*Halloween*, *Scream*, and *Nightmare on Elm Street*."

Madison shuddered. She has a weak stomach for scary movies. "Can we get *It's the Great Pumpkin, Charlie Brown*?"

"You'll be fine," I said.

Then we went to work on the invitation list. Haley, Serena, and Lauren were definitely in, as well as Bethany and Kelly from basketball. "Who else?" asked Madison.

Let's invite Harrison, I thought. Just the thought of it made my stomach do flip-flops. *What kind of present would I want Harrison to give me?* I must have gotten a seriously goofy look on my face because Madison gave me a strange look. I quickly rearranged my expression.

"We should also invite Talent," said Madison thoughtfully. "She would really like that."

I rolled my eyes. "Why don't we go ahead and invite my good friend Sloane Connors while we're at it?" I complained.

Madison pretended to write down Sloane's name. "Will madam be needing an engraved invitation?"

"Oh, indeed—I don't see any other possible way," I responded in my haughtiest voice, but thinking about Sloane made my voice quaver, just a little.

"Let's send it in poison ink," suggested Madison. Then she added, "Seriously, though, Lucy. Talent thinks we're her friends."

I sighed. "Can we talk about her later?" After lunch, Talent had to mention Chinese school to me about five more times. *Are you excited about going to Chinese school? We're already planning a harvest festival with mooncakes and everything!*

"Okay." Madison wrote down Talent's name with a

star next to it. "But I won't forget, and you'll be seeing her at Chinese school, so you won't, either."

Suddenly, something clicked. *Chinese school.* Maybe this was my ticket out of the free-throw contest and more skirmishes with Sloane.

"Listen, I've been thinking . . . with Chinese school and all, I'm not going to be on the basketball team this season. So, maybe I shouldn't go out for captain at school." I said it quickly, to get it over with.

Madison looked surprised. "Really? You really think that? 'Cause, you know, most of the kids who will be playing don't even play in a league. Look at Sloane."

Exactly—look at Sloane. "Yeah, I know, but . . . I just wouldn't have my best game if I wasn't in practice with Coach Mike and you guys. I mean, sure, I can do the free throws, but as far as leading the team, I wouldn't have my head in it." It wasn't a lie, exactly. It *could* have been true. It could have been a good reason not to go out for captain. It just wasn't the truth.

Madison thumped her pen against her lower lip, looking at the ceiling. "You would make a great captain."

I thought about how proud I had felt when Madison had pointed at me and mouthed *you*. I wondered what she would think if she knew the truth. "I think it's the right thing to do," I said.

Madison looked so disappointed that I could hardly look at her.

"If something comes up and I can go to basketball, I'll try out. Really," I added lamely, trying to cheer her up. *Yeah, like if Chinese school is destroyed by a meteor.*

Madison nodded, not saying anything. She picked up the notebook where we had been writing down all our party plans. "Now be honest, Lucy . . ." she began. I froze, waiting to be called out on the real reason I didn't want to go out for captain.

"Don't you think we can do better than hot dogs this year?" Madison smiled.

"For the party?" I exhaled. "Definitely." I didn't care if Madison wanted to serve bologna sandwiches and, ugh, blueberries. I just wanted to get past this moment, and have everything, *everything* get back to normal.

CHAPTER THIRTEEN

On Saturday, Regina came home for the day to see Yi Po.

Regina already seemed more grown-up, even though she had only been gone a month. She was wearing jewelry I'd never seen before, and she talked about *Econ* and *Poli-Sci*. Regina also brought a present for Yi Po, a scarf with the Hamilton University logo on it.

Yi Po thanked her, and then the two of them were off and running, chatting in Chinese a mile a minute. It was like they'd known each other forever. I wondered if Regina felt like a relief to Yi Po after Kenny, who spent more time eating than talking, and me. Maybe she wished that Regina were her roommate instead.

We went out for a great big Chinese lunch. My parents ordered tons of food because Regina complained that there were no good Chinese restaurants around Hamilton, and we spent most of the afternoon in a food coma. Regina came upstairs to look at our bedroom.

"The new wall color is nice," she said. "But a wall in the middle? Really, Lucy."

"I like it this way," I told her.

"If you kept your side a little neater, at least, the space wouldn't seem so small," said Regina. My side was currently decorated in a style I called, *I Can't Find My Math Homework.*

I didn't say anything as we walked back downstairs. We hung out some more, Dad gave Regina some money, and then at five o'clock, her ride picked her up to whisk her back to Hamilton.

"Why couldn't you stay for the weekend?" asked Mom, as Regina got ready to leave.

"I have to study," said Regina, "and besides, where would I sleep?"

After Regina left, the house felt funny. We had gotten used to Regina being away, and now we missed her all over again. Dad decided to go for a walk, and Yi Po went with him. I decided to go to my room while I had the chance to have it to myself.

My room is fifteen linoleum tiles wide by twenty tiles long, which means that my side of the room is seven and a half tiles wide. I can't even get to the bottom of the bookshelf that is part of the wall because of all the stuff I have piled up.

Looking at the wall now, though, I realized that the wall was on *my* half of the room, taking up part of *my* seven and a half tiles. The wall should be in the exact middle, along the eighth row of tiles, just to be fair. That would give me a whole extra half row of tiles for space.

I knew that if I tried to bring this up with Yi Po, one of two things would happen. One would be that she would start looking confused halfway through my sentence and then whatever little bit of Chinese was in my mouth would shrivel up and die. The other would be that she would get my parents to explain and then it would become a great big deal. And I'd probably get yelled at in the process for being a bad host, having a bad attitude, blah blah blah.

It would just be easier to quietly sl-i-i-i-de the book-case over the necessary few inches, wouldn't it? Yi Po would never notice, and Mom wouldn't hear me down-stairs if I was very, very careful.

I grabbed one end of the bookcase and slid it over. *Thump.* A couple of books tipped over and fell out. I held my breath and waited a minute to see if Mom was going to yell something up the stairs. She didn't.

I picked up the other end of the bookcase and slid it over so that it lined up neatly with the other end, along the eighth row of tiles. Oh, yeah—that was *so* much better.

Now for the desk. The desk was going to be kind of a problem because I didn't technically use my desk as a desk since the wall went up. It was more like the place where I put my not-that-dirty clothes, homework, protein bars, games, and other stuff I wanted to keep track of. Moving *that* without causing an avalanche was going to be tough.

I pulled as carefully as I could on the desk, but it shuddered along the floor. *Thud-a-thud-a-thud.* A stack of slick magazines slid forward, right to the edge. A mug of old hot chocolate threatened to jump off the desk.

I pushed everything back toward the center of the desk, trying to leave a wide margin along all sides for spillage.

"Lucy!" Mom yelled from downstairs. "Come set the table for dinner."

"Coming!" I yelled back.

I gave the last corner of the desk one hard pull, and the desk slid over into its new position without anything falling off. As I walked out the door, I gave the room one last look — seven tiles for my side, one tile for the wall, and seven tiles for Yi Po. Now that was fair.

I SPENT THE NEXT AFTERNOON OVER AT MADISON'S house, shooting hoops and watching movies. Mrs. Jameson ordered a pizza for dinner and invited me to stay, so I didn't get home until dark. Yi Po had already gone to bed — it was early, even for her.

But even in the dark, I could see that something was different. I pushed the door open a tiny bit wider, and counted the tiles. Sure enough.

Now there were six tiles on my side, one in the middle for the wall, and eight on Yi Po's side.

Had I miscounted before? Missed a row? That seemed impossible. Which left just one other possibility: Yi Po had done it herself.

For a moment, I felt indignant. *She moved the wall!* But then, I couldn't help smiling. I was busted, plain and simple.

I'd put the wall back in the middle tomorrow when no one was looking, and put it back to the old way, just so we'd have an understanding.

I hated to admit it, but the whole thing made me like her, just a little.

CHAPTER FOURTEEN

WHEN MOM COMES TO SCHOOL TO PICK ME UP, SHE always does something embarrassing, like talk too long to the teacher or wave to every single kid she knows. One time she parked in the bus line and held up all the buses until she moved her car.

This time, though, she broke all the records. Right as we were lining up to go to art, Mom appeared at the door. "Lucy! Time to see the dentist!" She made a motion like she was brushing her teeth with a giant toothbrush.

Mrs. Tibbs's class was walking by when she did it. I heard Sloane laughing. "Time to see the dentist! Time to see the dentist!" she said, mimicking Mom. "Gotta brush my great big teeth!" She didn't say it loudly, but it was like my ears had a special frequency just for Sloane. A burst of Amazon giggles followed.

I grabbed my backpack and shoved my homework inside, hoping to keep Mom from doing anything else. "See ya," I muttered to Madison.

"Three more days until Chinese school!" Talent trilled from her seat.

I gave Talent the instant-death stare. She shut up.

It should be three more days until basketball practice. That's how things should be.

I trudged after Mom through the parking lot. Mom was either completely unaware of how annoyed I was, or she was trying to cheerfully chatter her way out of it. "Look at those gorgeous flowers!" She pointed at the patch of flowers in blue and yellow, our school colors. "I guess we have the PTA to thank for that."

You can thank the president of the PTA for a lot more than that, I thought, *like her precious daughter Sloane making my life miserable.*

Mom didn't notice that I wasn't actually participating in the conversation. She went on and on about the new school sign, the upcoming gift-wrap fund-raiser, and the bake sale. It was like she had never been to my school before. She never mentioned anything about the sixth-grade basketball game.

Mom had no clue what was going on. Like Sloane.

Like basketball. Like my birthday party. She hadn't said anything about what would happen to my party with Yi Po being here.

"So where are you taking Yi Po on Halloween weekend?" I asked suddenly.

Mom was concentrating on backing out of the parking space. "What? Lucy, what are you talking about?"

"You know. Halloween — Madison and I are having our joint party that weekend, so Yi Po will have to go out, right?" I thought about the row of tiles in my room. "You could take her somewhere really nice. Like Belleview Gardens."

"It's not a great time to go away for the weekend," said Mom. "But if you and Madison wanted to have a small party in the afternoon at our house on Halloween, that would be fine."

I think Kenny gets his cluelessness from Mom, in addition to his math genes. Who wants a small afternoon party on Halloween? "It . . . won't . . . be . . . the . . . same," I said very slowly, like you would talk to a little kid. "The best parties on Halloween are at *night*, and they're *big*."

"Well, honey, that won't work because Yi Po is here," said Mom calmly.

"*Of course* it won't work," I snapped. I turned and stared out the window. "It's just one more thing that this whole visit has ruined." I felt tired, like everyone in the world was picking on me.

"Maybe we could . . ." she started, but I interrupted her.

"Never mind. We'll just have it at Madison's house."

Mom took a deep breath. I was expecting her to start yelling at me any second, but instead, she surprised me.

"You know, Lucy, you've been walking around with a pretty big chip on your shoulder. You had all these expectations about what this year was going to be like, and now it's turning out different."

"Tell me something I don't know."

We were at a red light, and Mom turned and looked at me. It was weird to look at her whole face. It was as if we were so busy these days that I only saw her in profile as she drove the car or cooked dinner. Her eyes were large and thoughtful.

"I know this has been hard for you, but I think you might try to figure out what good things might come out of the situation as it is. Stop wishing for things to be different, and take them as they are."

"That's easy for you to say," I said. "Absolutely *nothing* has gone my way since Yi Po got here. I have to go to this stupid Chinese school instead of basketball. I barely got to enjoy my own room, and it *smells* now, and . . ."

I hesitated. I had almost said something about Sloane Connors, but then I replayed the image of Mom standing in the classroom doorway, pretending to brush her teeth. There was a very good chance that telling Mom about Sloane would only make things worse, not better.

"Everything is just messed up," I said.

Mom didn't say anything. Was she even listening?

EVEN WITH PERFECT TEETH, I DON'T EXACTLY *LIKE* going to see the dentist, but as far as dentists go, Dr. Espinoza is pretty nice. Her daughter Marilisa was on my team last year, and it was funny to see her at practices in

146

her nondentist clothes. Dr. E. likes to put photographs and artwork on the walls and ceilings so that the patients have something to look at while she's cleaning their teeth. It almost makes me forget about the weird back-of-the-nose antiseptic smell that all dentist offices seem to have.

This time, I noticed that she had long mobiles made of different colored silk leaves. When you look up at them, you feel like you are under a tree.

"'ice 'o-eel," I said, pointing at the mobile.

"Thank you!" said Dr. E., reaching for a little mirror. "I got them at a craft fair." They must have a class in dentist school on how to understand people when their mouths are wide open.

"Are you ready for basketball season?" she asked.

I shook my head, barely. "'o. I ha' 'hi-ese s'ool." I tilted my head back and raised my voice so Mom could hear me in the waiting room. "'y 'arents are 'aking 'e go!"

"Chinese school, huh?" Dr. E. shook her head sympathetically. "Yeah, it's always something. We're skipping basketball because the games conflict with Marilisa's confirmation classes."

"See, Lucy?" Mom called back from the waiting room. "Everyone's got something." I made a face. The reflection in Dr. E.'s glasses scowled back.

Dr. E. put her tools down and picked up some floss. "Hey, did you hear Coach Mike is having a baby?"

I raised my eyebrows to show happy surprise. Coach Mike and his wife, Jenny, had been trying to have a baby for a couple of years. No one had ever told us, of course, but at the games, the moms would gather around Jenny and you'd hear words like *IVF* and *hormone injections*.

Dr. E. nodded enthusiastically. "They're quite excited, of course. And I just heard they're moving up practice to eight-thirty so they can make birthing classes." She laughed and reached for some floss. "*That* would be hard for Marilisa, let me tell you."

I could barely breathe. Basketball practice was at eight-thirty? That meant I could go to basketball practice *and* still make Chinese school by ten. A few days ago, I would have leaped out of the dentist's chair and done cartwheels down the hall. Now, my words to Madison came back to me. *If something comes up and I can go to basketball, I'll try out. Really.*

"Are you in pain?" asked Dr. E. I suddenly remembered that I was in the dentist's chair.

I shook my head and she handed me some water to rinse with. *Pain?* I thought. *You have no idea.*

WHEN I GOT HOME FROM THE DENTIST'S OFFICE, THERE was an excited message from Madison with the same news — *Coach Mike's wife is pregnant, and practice time was moved up!* She was yelling so loud that you could hear the answering machine all over the house. My mind spun in a hundred different directions. I had gotten what I had wanted — a chance to play hoops in spite of Chinese school — and now I wasn't so sure. Completing the sixth grade, pain-free, seemed like a much better idea.

Maybe my parents would *still* say that I couldn't play basketball — that would take care of everything. Yes, now I was hoping that my parents would become strict and unsupportive.

Before I could even think of what to say, though, Mom walked in and put her hand on my arm.

"I heard, Lucy. Yes, you can go now since it doesn't interfere with Chinese school. Why don't you call Madison with the good news?" She grinned at me, waiting for me to jump up and down and thank her. I guess she had been listening to me in the car, after all.

What a rotten time for Mom to become an overly sympathetic parent.

I DID MY BEST TO SOUND EXCITED WHEN I CALLED Madison about basketball. The first part was easy—YES, I was definitely excited about getting to play for the team and Coach Mike again. The second part, the tryout for captain, was a little harder.

"Should I start calling you Captain now, or wait until it's official?" teased Madison.

Um, why don't you wait until Sloane is done kicking my butt?

CHAPTER FIFTEEN

I COULD HEAR THE SQUEAK OF SNEAKERS AND THE *thump-thump* of balls before I even reached the gymnasium. In spite of my doubts, a thrill rippled through me and I couldn't help grinning. No matter what else happened, I felt like I belonged here more than any place on Earth.

Coach Mike blew the whistle. "Let's warm up!"

For the first time in days, I forgot about Yi Po, Sloane, and messed-up birthday parties. Coach Mike worked us like dogs. "Come on, you have another set of sit-ups after these push-ups!" he said cheerfully, twirling his lanyard around his finger. "You guys have got to get in shape!"

After warm-ups, we ran drills. Passing drills, shooting drills, dribbling drills. It seemed like Coach Mike had spent his summer learning about a hundred new drills to run us through. I felt like my arms were about to fall off during a free-throw drill, when Coach Mike walked by.

"Nice free-throw technique, Lucy! I can see some-one has been working this summer!" he bellowed, loud enough for the whole team to hear.

That gave me a burst of energy, though not enough for the last drill of the day. At that point, we were all panting and sweating. Half the girls were doubled over and the other half were gulping down water.

Coach Mike looked at us and rubbed his hands together. "Now for everyone's favorite—suicides! Let's go!"

They're not called suicides because they're pleasant. You start on one end of the court, and you run up to the near free-throw line and back. Then you run to half-court and back, the far free-throw line and back, and then the far end of the court and back. You don't jog during suicides—you run like a maniac but with enough control that you can stop and turn when you're supposed to.

The team groaned but Coach Mike rolled his eyes. "One if you're fast, two if you're slow!" he announced.

"I can't believe he's making us do this," I whispered to Madison. "I'm dying."

Madison grinned. "Yeah, but it beats missing basketball completely, doesn't it?" And then, in case I'd forgotten, she added, "And now you'll be totally prepared to take down Sloane."

Coach Mike blew the whistle to start and I took off running for the free-throw line. What I wanted to do, though, was run through the doors, out of the school, and far, far away.

As soon as practice was over, Mom was outside waiting in the car. Mom shook her head when she saw me. "I can't believe you're going to Chinese school like this! What will your teachers say?" she lectured as I got in the car.

Of course she's not interested in how practice went. I leaned over and looked in the rearview mirror. I had to admit that I was not about to make the world's best first impression. My face was bright red and my hair was straggly with sweat. I also wore an old T-shirt that boasted two holes and a faded brown spot from a bad encounter with some barbecue sauce.

I started fixing my ponytail, then gave up. There was no point. "I'm going, right?" I said. "I don't want to go, but I'm going."

Mom looked at me in the rearview mirror. "That's enough, Lucy. I thought getting to play basketball would take away some of this attitude."

As if. I wanted to tell her that getting to play basketball while still going to Chinese school was like getting a brand-new car that you only got to drive to work. On Saturdays.

"I think this is the right street," she said more to herself than to me as she turned right.

Forest Hills High School loomed into view, and from the looks of it, every Chinese family in a fifty-mile radius was there. They were all heading into the main set of doors.

Mom pulled up to the curb. "Hop out. The parking here is a nightmare. I'll catch up with you after I park."

Suddenly, I felt a surge of panic. What if I didn't understand what they wanted me to do? What if my Chinese was so bad they put me in a class with babies?

"Umm . . . I think I'll just stay in the car and go in with you," I said, trying not to let my panic show.

"Don't be silly, Lucy," Mom said impatiently. "Go. You're going to be late."

I stepped out of the car slowly and trudged up the steps into the main hall of the school. There were long lines of people extending from a row of tables. I found the table marked T-Z and got in line.

"*Ming zi?*" demanded a sour-looking man when I reached the end of the line.

"*Wu Mengxue,*" I answered, feeling pleased that I knew he was asking for my name.

Unfortunately, it went downhill from there. He flipped through a stack of papers, pulled out one. He started asking me questions in rapid-fire Chinese.

Some of the questions I understood, but I couldn't figure out how to answer in Chinese. Other questions, I only recognized some of the words, but not the whole question. I was drowning in wave after wave of Chinese words and phrases. *Should I fess up? Should I explain that I can't understand?* I looked around for Mom, hoping she could explain. No Mom. He was starting to look kind of mad when I felt a hand gently grip my arm.

What's the matter? I heard someone ask in Chinese.

The man stopped looking mad and started explaining, smiling, and pointing down the hall. I turned to see who had saved me from certain doom.

It was Talent Chang.

Talent kept a grip on my arm until she had steered me clear of the registration table. Then she released my arm and wiped her hand on her pants.

"Eeewww. How can you be so sweaty at . . ." She glanced at her watch. "10:07 in the morning?"

"Basketball practice," I said. Even with her obnoxious comment, I was fairly certain this was the happiest I'd ever been to see Talent. Or ever would be.

"Yech. Have you ever heard of a towel?" Talent, of course, was dressed as Little Miss Junior Chinese School Administrator. She was wearing a blue and white striped oxford and chinos, crisply ironed.

"I didn't know the coach was going to work us so hard today," I replied, feeling sheepish. Normally, I would have had a snappier comeback—*have you ever heard of a T-shirt and jeans?*—but I was too much out of my element. Throngs of kids, all Chinese, were passing us, and *they* all seemed to know what they were doing. I, on the other hand, was at the mercy of Talent Chang.

"Listen." Talent was walking at a brisk pace and I was jogging slightly to keep up. My calves ached, reminding me that I had already had my workout today. "They want you to go and meet with Professor Pao, so she can assess you and figure out what classroom is best for you. We've got to hurry, though, because she's getting really backed up over there, and you're going to miss the whole first day of class if you don't get in line soon."

"Okay." I was surprised by how much Talent cared. I thought she had been trying to get me to go to Chinese school just so she could show off.

She finally stopped at a classroom door. There were four people standing in line. Inside, I could see a plump older woman with glasses sitting on one side of a desk. "This is it," Talent announced crisply.

Talent spun around and headed back to the main hall. "Good luck," she said.

"Thanks," I said. "I mean, *xie xie*."

Talent looked back and gave me a look of approval. Somehow, Talent's know-it-all attitude didn't seem so horrible here. In fact, here, it kind of worked.

My interview with Professor Pao went better than I thought it would. I managed to carry on a very brief conversation in Chinese regarding the color of my shoes and the weather. My problem was that I couldn't always think of the word I wanted to use when I wanted to use it. I did recognize the characters for the numbers one, two, and three. Well, okay, to be fair, the characters for one, two, and three are one horizontal line, two horizontal lines, and three horizontal lines.

Professor Pao handed me a slip of paper with a room number on it. "Your accent isn't bad — you should work on vocabulary and idioms," she said sternly. "Practice!"

I nodded and took the slip of paper. Room 303. I needed to find a stairwell and go up two flights. The clock in the cafeteria said it was 10:45. Another hour and fifteen minutes of Chinese school—how was I going to survive? My steps slowed to a crawl.

Eventually I couldn't delay any longer and found Room 303. I opened the door without knocking. The desks had been rearranged in a circle and everyone was laughing and talking. A woman dressed in a gold jacket and burgundy skirt stood up and walked over.

"Hello! What is your name? *Wo shi* Jing Lao Shi," she said cheerfully. Her English was slowed by her accent and her effort to pronounce the words properly. I also noticed that instead of calling herself *Miss* or *Mrs.* Jing, she used the title of teacher, *lao shi*.

"*Wu jiao Wu Mengxue.*" I mumbled, surprised by how friendly she was.

"Welcome, Mengxue. I am so glad you are my student. Come sit. We are acting out the stories to Chinese idioms." She led me over to one group, two girls and one boy. They all turned and stared at me.

"Hey," I said.

"This is Wu Mengxue," said the teacher, putting one

arm around me, squeezing. "Please include her in your group." She grinned. "Be nice! She's the newest student in the class." She giggled like crazy at her own joke.

"Here," said the boy, handing me a sheet of paper. "We're acting out the story of *dong shi xi su*."

In my mind, I had planned to use the Amelia Helprin strategy in a large group, while the teacher was calling on me. Now the plan seemed less certain.

"I don't know this phrase," I said in my best wooden Amelia voice.

"Then hurry up and read the sheet," said the taller of the two girls impatiently. "C'mon, she's going to call on us in twenty minutes."

I glanced down at the sheet. We were supposed to act out our version of *dong shi xi su*, a Chinese phrase that means eating in the east and sleeping in the west. The original story was about a girl who had a choice between marrying two men. The guy who lived in the west was poor but handsome, and the guy who lived in the east was rich but ugly. People now use the phrase to describe someone who wants things both ways, like the girl wanted a good-looking boyfriend except when it came time to eat—then she wanted the rich guy who could buy her a fancy meal.

The two girls were arguing over who was going to play the girl, because neither one of them wanted to play a boy. The taller girl, Jessie, won out because she had a funny idea. "See, I'm going to put up my hand like this"—she put up her hand like a traffic cop and swiveled her shoulders—"and say, 'Don't make me look at you, just pass the lobster!' "

I started to laugh, but then stopped as soon as I realized Jing Lao Shi was looking at me. *No emotion, like Amelia*, I reminded myself. I dropped my eyes and looked at the handout again.

The other girl, Liane, said she would be the boy from the west. "If I have to be a boy, I'm going to be a good-looking boy," she announced. Adam, the only boy in the group, said he didn't care if he played the rich-but-ugly guy.

"I guess you can do a little intro, okay?" said Jessie to me.

I made one last attempt at Ameliadom. "I don't want to," I said. Jessie looked exasperated.

"I don't know what your problem is," she said heatedly. "And I don't care. I don't care that you don't want to. My parents have promised me a video phone if I get a good grade here and *you are not going to mess it up*! If you keep me from getting my video phone . . ."

"*Jiang zhongwen,*" Jing Lao Shi called over gently. *Speak Chinese. Yes,* I thought, *please threaten me in Chinese.*

I practiced the intro. *Once upon a time in China, there was a girl with two boyfriends. One was ugly but rich, one was poor but handsome.* I was a little nervous about some of the words, but Adam helped me out. "It's not hard, see?" he said. "*Rich* is *you qian,* you have money. *Poor* is *mei you qian,* you have no money. *Ugly* is *hen nan kan*—difficult to look at!" He made a weird noise, which I guess was his way of laughing. It sounded like a cross between a dying lawn mower and a donkey. *Guh-huh, guh-huh.*

My whole act-like-Amelia plan was replaced by the

act-like-a-terrified-twit plan when it was time to perform. My voice trembled as I tried to keep track of the words I was supposed to use. When Jessie, Adam, and Liane took over, I breathed a sigh of relief.

I thought we did a pretty good job. Jing Lao Shi laughed when Jessie said her line, and no one else did anything funny with their story.

For homework, Jing Lao Shi told us to study all of the idioms we had used, and get used to using them in conversation. Then she stood by the door and said good-bye, adding some encouragement or praise to each student. "You were so funny!" she told Jessie. She told Adam he was so lucky to be in a group with three beautiful girls, and he blushed. When I passed her, I kept my eyes on the floor.

"Hey, Wu Mengxue," she called, patting me on the shoulder. "Good job today! Don't be so shy, okay?"

I glanced at her out of the corner of my eye and looked away. *"Zai jian,"* I said under my breath. *Good-bye.*

I walked out of the room and down the hall as fast as I could go without running. *Where was Mom? How fast could I get out of here?*

I turned the corner to get to the stairs and ran smack into Harrison Miller.

CHAPTER SIXTEEN

"HARRISON? WHAT ARE YOU DOING HERE?" I WAS SO surprised I sounded more like I'd found him in the girls' bathroom.

"Hey, Lucy." When Harrison smiled I noticed that he had a dimple on only one side of his face. "Nice to see you, too."

There was an awkward pause as my brain desperately tried to go from surprised mode to intelligent conversation. "So . . . what *are* you doing here?" I said feebly as I lowered my notebook slightly to cover the barbecue stain on my shirt. *Why hadn't I brushed my hair?*

"Ummm . . . I'm going to Chinese school?" Harrison had the tone of someone who is puzzled that the answer isn't obvious. "I'm here to practice my Chinese."

"Wait. You go here? You want to *practice* your Chinese? You *already speak* Chinese?" Harrison might as well have announced that he could fly around the room by flapping his arms.

Harrison gave me a strange look. "I thought everybody knew," he said. "My mom is Chinese. We don't speak too much Chinese at home, so we both thought it would be a good idea to sign up for this, at least until soccer next spring."

I tried not to stare directly at Harrison's face by pretending to be fascinated by the trophy case behind him. Was Harrison really Chinese? I studied his face with quick side glances. His eyes had the slightest hint of the single eyelid fold like many Chinese. And his hair was very dark and straight. How had I not noticed this before?

I thought of something to say, something that didn't make me sound like an idiot. "My mom and dad are making me come here. I hate it."

Harrison looked at the floor and smiled. "I wouldn't exactly say I hate it. My mom's sister is teaching here so it's kind of a family-type thing for me to come."

"Who is your mom's sister?" I had a very strange feeling in my stomach, like I already knew the answer.

"I call her Ai Yi. But her last name is Jing."

Omigod! My mind raced back over the class. How horrible had I been? Was Harrison's aunt going to tell him to stay away from me? Suddenly, I realized that I was still in my sweaty, bottom-of-the-drawer clothes from basketball practice. I could just see Harrison and Jing Lao Shi talking. At home. In Chinese.

Jing Lao Shi: *All my students are so lovely except for one. Miss Wu showed up in dirty, sweaty clothes and barely tried to speak Chinese.*

Harrison: *I know her! Ha! That's nothing compared to the bonehead things she's said in front of me.*

Jing Lao Shi: *I think you should stay away from her.*

Harrison: *Yeah—if she were in the east or west I would definitely go NORTH!*

"Lucy!" Mom walked toward me and Harrison. "I've been waiting for you downstairs for ten minutes! I thought you couldn't wait to get out of here."

Aaack! My feet suddenly took on a life of their own and propelled me down the hall. If Mom met Harrison today, then the next time she showed up at school she'd be giving him the social third degree.

"Gotta go. See you," I said, not too loudly.

"Good to see you. *Zai jian*," Harrison responded. His Chinese accent was perfect.

"Who was that boy you were talking to? Is he part of the Chinese school?" Mom asked as we walked out to the car.

"A boy from my school and yes." I hoped that quick, short answers would keep her from asking too many more questions. Then, to answer the question I knew was coming next, I said, "He's part Chinese." *He had said, "Good to see you." He was glad to see me! Harrison Miller was glad to see me!*

"Ohhhh," Mom said. "Interesting."

She didn't say anything else. I slid into the seat and for one moment, enjoyed the feeling of the sun-warmed seat and the gorgeous white clouds playing across the bright blue sky.

"So, how was your first day of Chinese school?" asked Mom.

"Not bad," I said softly. Not bad, indeed.

ON SUNDAY, MOM, YI PO, AND I WENT TO OVERSTONE Mall. We don't normally go there because Fairleaf Shops are closer, but Mom thought that Yi Po would enjoy seeing the fancier mall with the huge aquarium and indoor garden.

Mom said she wouldn't buy me anything, but when we walked by Kicks, my favorite shoe store, I dragged Mom and Yi Po inside with me. Kicks has the best selection of basketball shoes around.

"You still have a pair from last season," Mom reminded me.

It's hard to resist the siren call of a new high-top, though. The right pair of shoes make you feel like you can jump an extra two feet. "Let's just look," I said.

They had one of those arcade basketball machines next to the basketball shoes. A man wearing a black-and-white striped referee shirt slapped the machine and said, "Hey there, little lady! Today I'm offering you a choice of either a fifteen-percent-off coupon, or a percent off for every basket you make in a minute."

Normally I can't stand the phrase *little lady* because it sounds so corny. But today, I had better things to think about.

"So, like, if I get twenty-five baskets in a minute, you'll take twenty-five percent off the shoe price?" I asked. Maybe Mom would get me a new pair of shoes if I got a big enough coupon.

The man leaned over and let out a loud bark of a laugh. "Sure," he said. "Go for it."

"Oh, Lucy," said Mom. "Just take the coupon. We'll save it for when we need it."

"No way," I said, and I picked up the first ball.

Yi Po tugged on Mom's arm and said, *"Ni kan." Watch.*

There were three balls in the machine and at first, I was shooting so fast that one ball would end up blocking the other. But I quickly found my rhythm and began throwing them in, nice and soft, one after the other. After five, I lost count and just focused on the basket. Everything just seemed to fade into the background. The clock seemed to go on for a long time.

Buzz!

The man looked at the scoreboard, gave the machine a little shake, and then looked at the scoreboard again. "Twenty-four," he said reluctantly when the score stayed the same.

I jumped up and down. "Woo-hoo!" I said. "Twenty-four! How 'bout that!"

"You don't *need* a new pair, though, right?" said Mom.

"Can I just look?" I begged.

"I think Yi Po would like to see the rest of the mall, and I know you'll want to study *all* the shoes," said Mom. "How about you stay here, and we'll be back in twenty minutes or so, okay?"

Maybe Mom would get me a new pair of shoes. "Sure, Mom," I said.

I watched other people come in the store and shoot baskets. No one even came close to my score, not even the six-foot-plus high school student who was showing off for his friends. *They* were impressed when he got a seventeen.

I narrowed my choices down to a pair of red and white high-tops, which would have looked great with my uniform, and a sleek pair of silver ones, when Gabi and Ariana showed up.

Gabi and Ariana were in my grade, and they used to be normal people — they even played ball a few years ago. Now they seemed to spend most of their time trying to look like each other. Today they both were wearing pink lip gloss, had their hair in pigtails, and had their sweatshirts zipped exactly halfway up.

Ariana gave Gabi a nudge and they both stared at me. "What are you doing?" Gabi asked me.

"Just getting some new shoes," I said, like it was no big deal. But I had a funny feeling. Gabi and Ariana were in Mrs. Tibbs's class, with Sloane.

"You're always doing something with basketball, aren't you?" asked Gabi. It almost sounded like an accusation.

I tugged at the hem of my T-shirt. "Not always. Sometimes."

The salesman walked over toward us. "You ladies want to try your luck at the machine? Your friend scored a twenty-four-percent discount today with some great shoot-ing." I guess he wasn't upset about my scoring anymore.

Gabi stared at him. "No . . ."

". . . thank you," finished Ariana. He gave them a funny look and walked away.

"You're good," said Gabi. "You must practice a lot."

"Thanks," I said, but inside I was racking my brain. *Was Sloane at the mall, too?*

I ran my hand over the shoes, feeling the smooth leather. *What should I do next?*

Suddenly, Gabi pointed out the storefront window. "Who is *that*?" she shrieked. She grabbed Ariana's arm.

I followed the direction of Gabi's arm and realized she was pointing at Yi Po, who at that moment was heading toward the Bathtastic store across the way.

I had kind of forgotten that she looked a little strange, with her wiry hair, missing tooth, and dark blue clothing. As Kenny put it, she didn't look *American*.

"Is that your grandmother?" asked Gabi.

"No!" The word popped out before I could sound a little less freaked out. I swallowed hard. "That is not my grandmother."

"Omigod, she's waving to us. How funny," said

Ariana. Yi Po was standing outside the store, giving me a little wave as if to say, *We're here now.* "C'mon, Lucy, she *must* know you, or why would she wave to you?" She waved back, though not in a perfectly friendly way. Gabi laughed and waved, too.

I closed my eyes and wished, for just a second, that I had American relatives like everyone else's. Ones who didn't stand out. Ones who spoke English and blended in perfectly.

But relatives who were like everyone else's weren't like my grandmother, either.

I opened my eyes. Yi Po had gone into the bath store. I prayed she wouldn't come over.

"Well, *that* was interesting," said Ariana. Gabi laughed like Ariana had just told the world's funniest joke. I tried to act as if I hadn't heard them.

"Yeah, well, I think I'm going to try these shoes on," I said. As though I needed to be alone to put on shoes.

"So, you're going out for captain of the basketball team at school," Gabi said abruptly.

My whole body felt like one giant *gulp*. This was definitely Sloane-related.

"I'm definitely maybe kind of possibly thinking about it," I said, trying to make a joke out of it.

Gabi and Ariana looked at each other, and then they both said, "Hmmm . . ."

"We have to be going," announced Gabi.

I stood in the middle of the store, not moving, until they were out of sight. Then I put the shoes back on the display. I didn't feel like getting shoes anymore.

When Mom and Yi Po came back to the store, Yi Po gestured toward the window and said something in Chinese. I caught the word *peng you*, or friends.

She probably thought all girls my age were my friends. I choked out the most basic words in Chinese: *They are not my friends.*

"What is Yi Po talking about, Lucy? Did you run into somebody here?" asked Mom.

I didn't answer, and Yi Po gave me a funny, almost sad look. But how could I explain this problem of my not-friends to my not-grandmother?

CHAPTER SEVENTEEN

ON MONDAY WHEN I GOT TO SCHOOL, I HAD TWO simultaneous thoughts: *Look for Harrison, avoid Sloane, look for Harrison, avoid Sloane.* Unfortunately, I couldn't look for Harrison because something blocked my view. Sloane.

"So, Lucy," said Sloane. She slid in front of me and cornered me between a table and chair. We were in the cafeteria, where they corralled us before class on rainy days. There was no escape. "I heard that your family has a *special visitor.*"

I tried to keep my face neutral. If only Madison were with me, instead of at the eye doctor this morning. "I don't know what you're talking about." But I knew. She was talking about Yi Po.

"Sure you do. At the mall. Who is she? Gabi and Ariana said she practically looked like a homeless person. All weird and stuff." Sloane poked her face close to mine and dropped her voice to a whisper. "I'd be really careful if I were you. I mean, it's really sweet that your family takes in homeless people, but people like that have all sorts of weird diseases. You wouldn't want to catch some terrible rash or head lice, would you?" The word *lice* echoed in my head. I thought of Kendra.

"It would be soooo terrible if you had to miss school, or even the big basketball game, because you had some *communicable disease*," cooed Sloane.

I looked at Sloane's face, her perfectly glossed mouth open in phony concern. I'm sure that to the cafeteria monitor, Sloane looked like the very picture of genuine caring.

"She's not a homeless person," I said shortly. It was all I could say and still be sure that my voice wasn't shaking.

"Then who . . ." started Sloane. But at that moment the bell rang, and the surge of students around us popped me free from Sloane's grip.

I walked to class feeling sick, not that I'd tell anyone that *now*. I could just see it — the minute I missed school, Sloane would gear up her nasty rumor machine. My breakfast churned inside my stomach, threatening to make an exit. *You should have just told her! You should have said, that was my aunt, and been done!* I told myself. Now I was doubly trapped between Sloane and something less than the truth, and I didn't like the way it felt, not one bit.

THE NEXT FEW WEEKS SPED BY. BASKETBALL SEASON GOT into full swing with Saturday and weeknight practices, and Ms. Phelps started assigning this-is-important-next-year-is-middle-school homework. On top of this, I was actually having to take Chinese school seriously.

Having Harrison's aunt as my teacher had called for a switch from Plan A to Plan B. Serious Plan B. Good-bye, Amelia Helprin — Hello, Regina Wu Junior! I actually studied the idioms Jing Lao Shi assigned to us and volunteered in class.

I also had to prepare for those few minutes after Chinese school when I saw Harrison. I wouldn't say that he was *waiting* for me, but he always seemed to be at the trophy case near my room after class. We never talked for long — I was too worried about an awkward pause that would ruin everything. But we talked about the cafeteria's first attempt at vegetarian meals—tacos with soy crumbles—homework assignments, and movies. We talked about our Chinese middle names—his was *Yulong*, Jade Dragon.

I also perfected the world's fastest makeover in the car after basketball practice:

1. Get in car, wipe self down with towel. (*Thanks, Talent!*)
2. Take hair out of ponytail, comb out hair. Check self in rearview mirror.
3. Pull nice shirt over practice shirt. Take off dirty shirt underneath. Do *not* let anyone see!
4. Change sneakers for cute shoes.
5. Put on tinted lip gloss and peach body spray. Sniff self. Check mirror again.
6. Jump out of car.

And on top of this, I had another assignment for regular school, Chinese school, and everywhere else: Be on guard against the Amazons at all times. I never walked home by myself and I always sat down *very* carefully.

But for those few weeks, nothing bad happened. Maybe Sloane had found something better to do, or, more likely, someone new to pick on. I started to think that if I put my head down and minded my own business, nothing else would happen.

MADISON'S BIRTHDAY CAME AND WENT, THEN EIGHT days before Halloween, I woke up to what seemed like a great day. I think it had something to do with finding my lucky Lady Vols T-shirt the night before. I thought I had lost it, but then I spotted the bright University of Tennessee orange at the bottom of my desk drawer. It listed all of the national championships the team had won with Pat Summitt. I started to feel excited about the student-faculty basketball game. It *would* be fun to design some plays and run the team, just like Pat. It would be really fun to win.

The day started with Yi Po actually sleeping in until 6:15, which meant that I got a decent night's sleep, too. My hair actually did what I wanted it to. Mom remembered to buy Cinnamon Snaps, my favorite cereal, and Dad gave Madison and me a ride to school because it was raining.

When I got to school, *more* great stuff happened. Ms. Phelps decided to cancel the social studies quiz on Monday, and when I walked down the hall past two Amazons, no one laughed. And Harrison went out of his way to say hi to me on the way to the pencil sharpener.

When I had to go to the girls' room at 10:15, I was practically floating on air. Then I found the writing on the wall.

If you don't flush
Lucy Wu
Will drink your pee
And stir-fry your poo.

Did it really say that? I shook my head and looked again. Still there. The wall seemed to grow until it was nearly flattening me. Sloane hadn't been leaving me alone—she had been plotting.

I grabbed some paper towels and tried to wash off the words with some soap and water. It didn't work. I wanted to kick the tile in, crack it, so no one else could see it. It reminded me of the chants that Mom had told me about — the horrible things that kids said to her when she was the only Chinese girl in the entire school. *Me Chinese, me play joke, me put pee pee in your Coke.*

My throat swelled and I felt tears threatening to spill over. *Don't cry, not here.* I heard someone walk into the bathroom, and I leaped back, terrified. *What if it was Sloane, or one of the other Amazons?* If they saw me crying, I might as well give up, put a big "Kick Me" sign on my back, and call it a day. Instead, I tried to look pissed off.

It wasn't Sloane. It was Talent, and I apparently did not look anything close to mad.

Her face softened as soon as she saw me. "Oh, Lucy," she said. "What's the matter?"

I swallowed and pointed at the tile. Talent bent down to read it.

"Do you know who wrote that?" she asked. She looked really mad.

I nodded. "I think so," I said in a small voice. Suddenly, I couldn't hold back any longer. I slid down the wall until my butt hit the floor, and then I let the tears come out. I buried my head in my arms to muffle any sound that would echo off the tile.

Talent waited. Through the little space between my arm and my leg, I could still see that her loafers were perfectly shined, and her socks matched her pants.

"I think it's Sloane Connors, or one of her friends," I finally choked out. "Sloane doesn't want me to go out for captain of the sixth-grade team."

Talent didn't say anything for a moment. Then she said, "That evil wi . . ."

"Excuse me?" The shock was enough to make me stop crying completely. I couldn't believe what I was hearing. The perfect Talent Chang?!

"I'm going to get the principal," announced Talent, heading for the exit.

I grabbed her arm. "Wait," I said. "Don't. Please don't."

"Sloane can't do this to us. This is an insult to all Chinese people."

Funny—I had never wanted to think of Talent and me as being an *us*, but at that moment I appreciated having someone on my side. Still, she had it wrong. "Sloane never had any problem with me before," I pointed out. "I think she would find something nasty to write if I were from—I don't know—*Finland*. It's not about where I'm from, where *we're* from—I just happen to be in the way of what she wants." I stood up and kicked the tile. "And I just want her to leave me alone."

"Mrs. Nicholson might be able to help you," said Talent. She still didn't get it.

"Listen," I said. "If you go and tell the principal, it will be like letting Sloane win."

Talent stared at me.

"Look, you need proof, right? No proof, no case. There's no way we can prove Sloane did this, or anything else, but if you go to Mrs. Nicholson, there will be a big stink, and I'll just look like a baby, going for help. If the Amazons figure out they're getting to me, I'm dead meat."

Talent nodded slowly.

"Promise me you won't tell anyone. Please."

She nodded again.

I pointed to the wall. "Do you have any idea how to clean that off? I tried soap, and it didn't work."

Talent reached down and opened her purse. It was a small brown leather purse, and it matched her belt and shoes perfectly. She pulled out one of those pens that is supposed to remove stains from clothing.

I stared at it for a moment. Talent fiddled with the cap, twisting it. "I don't like having soiled clothes," she said defensively. "It has bleach. It might work."

We tried rubbing it on the tile. It worked, not perfectly, but well enough that we erased most of the words, including my name and the part about stir-fried poo.

"We better go," said Talent. "We've been in here for a while."

"Okay." I put the cap back on the pen and handed it to Talent. Then I thought of something. "Do you have any plans for Halloween?"

Talent shook her head shyly. It suddenly occurred to me that she was probably one of those kids who went trick-or-treating alone. Or maybe she didn't go at all.

"You have plans now," I told her. "And you just might have to wear jeans."

She smiled.

CHAPTER EIGHTEEN

SLOANE'S CHANT GOT STUCK IN MY HEAD AND PLAYED over and over, drowning out everything around me. *If you don't flush . . .*

At practice, I missed the setup for an inbounds play. Twice.

Coach Mike blew his whistle. "Let's end practice with a double set of suicides, thanks to Miss Wu!"

The whole team groaned. That would be twelve times up the court and back. I think even Madison frowned at me.

Lucy Wu . . . will drink your pee . . .

Chinese school wasn't any better. Jessie was my conversation partner, and she snapped at me every time I pronounced something wrong. "What's the matter with you? Are you deaf?" she demanded. "You better not mess this up!"

"I know," I said, tiredly. "Or no video phone."

And stir-fry your poo . . .

Harrison didn't show up at our usual spot after Chinese school, either.

When I got home, all I wanted to do was crawl into bed and stay there for a long time. I hadn't been alone for five minutes when Yi Po came in. I scrunched down farther under the covers and pretended to be asleep.

She didn't buy it. *"Eh, Mei Mei, ni bu su fu ma?"* She wanted to know if I was feeling sick. I shook my head.

She put her hand on my forehead. Then she left without saying anything.

When my grandmother was alive, she did all sorts of things when I was sick. I tried to think of five things. She made honey-and-lemon drinks if my throat hurt. She folded scraps of paper into little animals and put them on trays of food she brought to me. She made my favorite sick food: steamed eggs with ground pork. She fussed over the blankets until she thought they were exactly comfortable for me.

That was only four. This made me feel worse. I could only think of four things—I was forgetting.

I must have fallen asleep because the next thing I knew, it was nearly dinnertime. My eyes were prickly with sleep, and I definitely felt like I needed a shower. As I got ready to go downstairs, I realized that my quilt had been neatly folded at the foot of my bed.

I unfolded the quilt. The tear had been re-repaired. Now the rip was disguised by a blooming branch of forsythia. The branch flowed into the other flowers in the quilt, though you could tell it was a little newer than the rest.

It had to be Yi Po. I found her in the family room, watching a cooking show and sewing a button on a shirt. I waited for her to look up, and then I held out the quilt. I didn't know how to say *repair* or *quilt*. Where to start?

She waved me off. *"Mei shi."* *No big deal.*

I stood in the family room, feeling shy. Then I sat down and watched the rest of the show with her.

CHAPTER NINETEEN

IN MY HOUSE, THERE ARE TWO KINDS OF FOOD—Chinese and American. American food is anything that isn't Chinese—whether it's Tex-Mex, Thai, or Italian. Before Yi Po showed up, we usually had Chinese food half the time, and American food half the time, which was just fine with me.

After Yi Po arrived, though, it was clear that we were going to have Chinese food all the time. At first it was because Mom was nervous about serving Yi Po anything except Chinese food. But then Yi Po slowly started to take over the kitchen, and of course, all she cooked was Chinese food. Mom protested, but the thought of coming home from work to a fully cooked dinner was an offer she couldn't refuse.

"This is *soo* wonderful," she murmured one night as she added another helping of cashew chicken into her bowl. "You all should be so thankful Yi Po is here because

I'm so slammed at work you'd be getting macaroni and cheese."

Macaroni and cheese? I thought. *I'd love some macaroni and cheese. Or lasagna. Or tacos.* Chinese food was okay, but not all the time!

When I told Madison about the all Chinese food, all the time situation, I didn't get the sympathetic reaction I was hoping for. "You are absolutely crazy," Madison informed me. "Invite me over for dinner."

"Okay," I said. "But only if I get some of your mom's fried chicken on a different day." Mrs. Jameson's chicken is so yummy you could just eat the crispy part and be happy.

When Madison came over for dinner, she threw her jacket on a chair and headed for the kitchen. "Let's find out what she's making."

I followed Madison into the kitchen. Yi Po was inside making dumplings.

"Hi!" Madison chirped. Yi Po looked at her and smiled. *Good luck with that*, I thought, *unless you suddenly know how to speak Chinese.*

Madison pretended to sniff the air and then rubbed her stomach. "Your food smells incredible!" she told Yi Po.

Yi Po's face lit up. She jumped out of her chair and went over to the stove. She spooned a dumpling out of a boiling pot of water into a little bowl and brought it over to Madison. She pointed to bottles of soy sauce and cider vinegar on the table, and Madison poured a little bit of each into her bowl.

Madison took her first bite. "This is amazing!" she shouted. "Have you ever had her dumplings?" she asked me. I shrugged. How much could you do with a dumpling?

"How do you say, *this is really good*?" asked Madison eagerly.

"Umm . . . you can say, *hao chi*," I said. "It means good to eat."

"Ho chee! Ho chee!" said Madison to Yi Po, pointing at her bowl with her fork. Even though my Chinese was not great, I could tell that Madison's accent was much worse.

Somehow, though, Yi Po understood what Madison was saying. She bobbed her head in a little bow and gave her a really big smile.

When we sat down to dinner, even I had to admit that Yi Po's dumplings were something special. Better than the dumplings Mom bought at the store, better than the ones at Panda Café. There were lots of different flavors in the filling—a little ginger, a little garlic, some sesame oil—and they all stood out and blended together in turns. Every bite left me wanting more.

Kenny, of course, was in heaven. Even though everyone was pigging out on the dumplings, I think Kenny ate more than everyone else combined. By the end, Kenny was leaning way back in his chair because he was so full, but still struggling to reach the ladle so he could have one more serving.

Madison nudged me. "Do you think your aunt would make these dumplings for our birthday party?"

Dumplings at a birthday party? No one had *dumplings* at a birthday party. You had pizza or hot dogs or tacos. Not *dumplings*.

"Do you think anyone will like them?" I asked doubtfully. I could just see it now—everyone wrinkling their faces at the dumplings and wishing they had pizza.

"How could anyone not *love* these dumplings? They are so delicious, and we can always order a pizza if someone has a fit," insisted Madison. "C'mon, ask her. *Puh-leeeze?*"

It was hard to say no when Madison looked so excited. And the party was at her house, *again*, so I felt like I owed her one.

"Um . . . Yi Po . . ." I began. Everyone else at the table stopped talking. I felt my cheeks start to burn. Yi Po stared at me.

"Wo men yao," I gulped awkwardly, pointing at Madison and myself, *"shui jiao . . ."* I was amazed I actually remembered the word for boiled dumpling—*shui jiao*. Now how did I say *party*?

Yi Po narrowed her eyes, Then she put her hands to one side of her head and closed her eyes. *"Shui jiao?"*

What did I do now? I looked helplessly at Mom and Dad. "I'm trying to ask Yi Po if she would make dumplings for our birthday party."

Mom smiled. "That was a nice try, Lucy. But you just told Yi Po that you and Madison wanted to sleep. Remember, *dumpling* uses third tone—*shui jiao*." Her voice glided up and down the words like a child on a swing. "*Sleep* is fourth tone." She repeated the words, but this time, her pronunciation changed to a sharper, downward ending.

I could hear the difference, but it seemed like every time I tried to say them, it came out wrong. My brain and tongue did not connect.

Mom leaned over and asked Yi Po if she would make dumplings for our birthday party. Yi Po looked at me and Madison, and nodded vigorously.

Madison squealed. "Thank you! Thank you! This is so awesome," she told Yi Po. Madison put her hand up and Yi Po reached up and slapped it. They both laughed. Great. Even my non-Chinese-speaking best friend could communicate with Yi Po better than I could.

CHAPTER TWENTY

A FEW DAYS LATER I CAME HOME FROM SCHOOL AND THE house was completely silent. No crackling radio, no *fwap-fwapp*ing slippers, nothing. Even Kenny wasn't around, performing his usual search-and-destroy mission on the refrigerator.

Aaaaah. I slipped my backpack from my shoulders, kicked off my shoes, and began to wander around the house. I hadn't had the house to myself in forever. I flipped on the TV and searched the pantry until I had found a snack-size bag of BBQ potato chips and an orange soda.

I settled into the beanbag chair and waited for one of my favorite decorating programs to come on, *Room for Improvement*. It's one of my favorite shows because they make all the changes for less than $500.

When *Room for Improvement* finished, I drained my soda and tossed the can into the recycling bin. It was 4:30 and Yi Po still wasn't home. Then I heard the door open.

I poked my head around the corner to see if it was her. It was Kenny instead. "Hey, Lucy, what's up?" Kenny strolled into the kitchen and grabbed a jar of peanuts.

"Yi Po wasn't here when I came home from school. Do you think we should be worried?" I asked him.

Kenny flipped a peanut into the air and caught it in his mouth. "Why? Do you think she was kidnapped?"

"No . . . but where could she have gone?"

Kenny shrugged. "Beats me. I wouldn't worry about it, though. How much trouble could she get into around here?" He tossed another peanut into his mouth.

An uneasy feeling filled my stomach—the same feeling that I got when Dad prepared to go on one of his business trips. *Maybe she got into a lot of trouble. Maybe she wandered outside and got hit by a car. Maybe she's in the hospital and no one knows how to help her. Maybe she's lost and can't read the signs.*

I reached for the phone. "I think I'll call Mom."

Before I could dial the numbers, though, the door opened again. It was Yi Po. A gust of wind blew the doorknob out of her hand. She quickly reached for the door and shut it.

She saw Kenny and me, and waved. She looked really happy. Then she went upstairs and into the bathroom.

My mind filled with questions. *Why do you look so happy? What have you been doing?* But I didn't know how to ask.

I asked Mom to find out where Yi Po went, but she was really busy with a project at work and forgot. I went to Dad after dinner.

"Dad," I said. "Yi Po went out somewhere today, and when she got home, she looked really happy. Where do you think she went?"

Dad grinned. "She tried to find a girlfriend for Kenny!" he said mischievously. Daddy had been in such a good mood since Yi Po arrived. He was always making jokes or bringing home little desserts. I think it was the food Yi Po was cooking for him.

That made me think of Harrison, and I blushed. "Be serious, Daddy," I said. "Don't you think we should be . . . you know . . . worried?"

Dad shook his head. "The women in your mother's family are very capable, you know. If she's happy, then I'm happy."

"But will you ask her where she went?" I persisted.

"Why don't *you* ask her, if it's that important to you?"

I shook my head. "I can't. Even when I know how to say the words, I'm afraid I'm not going to say them right. You know, I could accidentally sound really rude or something. And, I probably wouldn't understand the answer, either."

Dad put his arm around me. "I think you're being a little hard on yourself, honey. Don't worry about getting it perfect. Just try, okay?"

I thought about the sleep/dumpling incident and sighed. I could just see all of our conversations becoming one giant misunderstanding.

"Never mind," I said.

THAT NIGHT, I WALKED PAST THE LIVING ROOM AS MOM, Dad, and Kenny started settling in for what had become their semiregular evening chat with Yi Po. Mom would fix a tray of tea and peanuts and other Chinese snacks, and they would talk for hours. It was one of the few times Kenny actually wanted to hang out with grown-ups. I leaned against the doorway. A piece of tile was coming loose on the floor.

"Hey, Lucy," said Dad. "Come join us. Don't be such a hermit."

I leaned against the doorway. "I've got a lot of homework."

"Since when do you care so much about homework? C'mon, stay for a few minutes."

I hesitated. "Okay—just a few." I walked into the living room and took the chair closest to the door.

Mom brought in the tray of drinks and snacks. Dad stretched out next to Kenny. "How are your Mathwhiz practices coming along?" Dad asked. Dad was so proud that Kenny was on the senior team, even though Kenny was only a sophomore.

Kenny looked away. "Fine," he said.

Yi Po was straightening a stack of books on the coffee table. That was something she did that reminded me of my grandmother. Her hands were never still—like hummingbirds. They were always in motion—cooking, cleaning, gesturing, knitting.

"She reminds me of Po Po when she does that," I said to Kenny. Kenny nodded. Then he said to Yi Po, in Chinese, *Do you remember her at all? You were so little when she left.*

Yi Po finished straightening the books and looked at Kenny. *I remember that we had three toys—a doll, a ball and—*she said a word I didn't know and twirled her index finger down, like a drill. She might have said spinning top. She suddenly scooped up the imaginary toys and held them greedily to her body. She laughed, and suddenly I could see her as a little girl, wanting all three toys for herself.

Yi Po said something else, and pantomimed giving someone a piggyback ride. I looked at Mom. Mom said, "She said that their mother used to carry Po Po to school on her back." Yi Po looked at me and pointed to her foot. Mom added, "Shoes back then were probably very delicate, handmade, you know. Very expensive. They wouldn't be able to stand up to daily walks over rocks and dirt roads."

I thought of our front hallway, piled with shoes—boots, sneakers, dress-up shoes, sandals. I thought about how I just *wanted* a pair of shoes at Kicks, even if I didn't need them.

Every morning, I was so mad that my sister went to school. I would cry. My aunt scolded me. Yi Po's expression transformed into that of the frustrated aunt, and she wagged her finger at an imaginary child. Then she said something else.

"What did she say?" I asked. No one said anything for a moment.

Dad looked pained. "They told her not to bother to cry, because no one cared about the tears of a girl."

Something inside me burned. I had known that in the old days, Chinese families favored boys and some still did, but who would say something so mean to a little kid? Then I remembered that this was the family Yi Po had been left with.

Do you remember anything else? asked Kenny.

Yi Po tilted her head to one side, thinking. *When she left I felt very*— she said a word I hadn't heard before, but I knew. Her eyes had lost their usual brightness.

When she left I felt very sad.

I stood up. "I have homework," I said quickly, and left the room before any more of her words would dig into me. For all those times I didn't understand what Yi Po was saying, this time I understood all too well.

Even after two years, there were times when my grandmother's death felt like a fresh cut. I missed her so much. If I could, I would have told Yi Po I felt the same, but all I had were clunky nouns and adjectives, and everyday phrases. *Red cup! Big desk! Let's eat!* I needed the small, delicate words that said: *I know how you feel. I miss her, too. She was special. She was irreplaceable.*

Before I went to bed that night, I thought of one thing I could do. I took my favorite picture of my grandmother, the one I had kept hidden in my bookcase, and put it on top of the wall. Facing her side.

CHAPTER TWENTY-ONE

HALLOWEEN ARRIVED AND IT WAS AN INCREDIBLY BUSY day. I had to go to basketball practice and Chinese school, and on top of that, I still had to get my costume ready. I was going as an order of French fries. I had taped together some sheets of red poster board for the box, but I still had to cut up some foam rubber for the fries. If you don't have a good costume when you're an older kid, you usually don't get as much candy and the adults give you dirty looks. You have to show that you're in the spirit of things.

Fifteen minutes before I was supposed to be at Madison's house, I finally lugged all my stuff downstairs to the front door. Even though Madison didn't live far away, Mom was going to give me a ride, since we had to bring the dumplings.

I ran over to the freezer to get out the dumplings. Mom and Yi Po had made them a few days ago and frozen them in plastic bags.

In the freezer there was one bag of dumplings.

"Moooooommm!" I yelled. "Where are the rest of the dumplings?"

"They're all together!" Mom yelled back. "They're all in the freezer together!"

I looked again. Two cartons of ice cream. A bag of peas. Mystery roast. Pizza. Four cans of frozen orange juice.

One bag of dumplings.

"I think we're going to go hungry if these are all the dumplings," I told Mom as she came into the kitchen.

Mom looked through the freezer herself, digging all the way to the back like an arctic explorer. No more dumplings.

She pulled her head out of the freezer and shouted one word. "KENNNNNYYY!"

Apparently Kenny had been helping himself to a nightly snack of dumplings when everyone else had been asleep. In his usual state of cluelessness, it never quite occurred to him that the dumplings had been for the party.

"What are we going to do?" I asked. "Order pizza?" I tried to sound disappointed, but truthfully, I was relieved. I liked the dumplings, and Madison liked the dumplings, but that didn't mean *anyone else* would like the dumplings.

Mom scratched her arm. "Well . . . that does seem to be the . . ." but before she could finish her sentence, Yi Po butted in.

We can do it! she said to Mom. She said some other things, but the only part I understood was, *Let's go to the store now!*

I held my breath, waiting for Mom to respond with something like, *No, no, it's too much trouble.* But that's not what she said.

"Yi Po says we cannot disappoint you or Madison. We'll drop you off at Madison's house on the way to the store," said Mom briskly. "Start loading the car."

I chewed on my lip. I knew she was trying to be nice, but Yi Po was messing up my party—again.

I GOT TO MADISON'S HOUSE TEN MINUTES BEFORE THE party started. Talent was already there.

"Um . . . hi, Talent," I said slowly. "Aren't you a little early?"

Talent had no clue that coming early to a party was not exactly the best idea in the world. "I made my mom bring me here straight from the mall, where I bought jeans! Look!"

This was probably the closest that Talent had ever come to looking like a normal person. She even had a T-shirt on. It had a picture of two cartoon kittens dancing under a rainbow.

"How long has she been here?" I asked Madison under my breath.

"Fifteen minutes," Madison whispered back. "But she's been really helpful."

I told her the news. "Kenny ate most of the dumplings that Mom and Yi Po made, but they're going to the store so they can make more." Then I paused. "Do you think we should order pizza? Just in case?"

"Nah," said Madison. "Look, we've got tons of chips and stuff if people are hungry." Then she whipped out a present. "Happy birthday, by the way."

I ran my fingers over the smooth wrapping paper. I love that moment right before the paper comes off, when the package is so pretty and there could be anything inside.

"Open it," urged Madison. "Then you can wear it for the party."

Madison's really good at picking out gifts that really match the person. Judging from the size of the box, it had to be jewelry. I tore off the paper and lifted the lid. Inside was a Chinese character on a silk cord. *Huh?*

"Like it?" Madison took it out of the box to tie around my neck. "I got myself one, too." Madison knew what it said and I didn't. Great.

Talent saved me. She pushed between us to get a look. "Oh! *Hu—lao hu*—tiger. I guess that's your zodiac sign, huh? I'm a rabbit."

I nodded numbly, trying to look happy instead of how I felt, which was stupid and irritated. What was up with Madison? First the dumplings, now the necklace. It was like *she* was trying to be Chinese.

"Here," I said, trying to cover up my disappointment. "It's your birthday, too." I handed her the present I had picked out for her — a T-shirt that said *Eat, Sleep, Shoot Hoops.*

By the time Mom and Yi Po got back to Madison's house, half of the people had arrived. Mom and Yi Po didn't bring in dumplings, though — they brought in grocery bag after grocery bag of *ingredients* for dumplings.

"I thought you were just going to make some more dumplings and drop them off," I said to Mom. I didn't want Yi Po hanging around the party, especially after the way Gabi and Ariana had made fun of Yi Po at the mall. Mom gave me a *look*. "Lucy, the grocery store was packed, and it does take a while to make all the dumplings. We'll work as fast as we can, but it'll be faster if we make them here, rather than try to make them at home and then bring them here."

I looked over at Madison and rolled my eyes. Madison shook her head to say, *No big deal.*

It was a big deal, though. The whole party was becoming a mess wrapped in a disaster covered in a mistake. Yi Po and Mom were here. Talent was hanging out by herself, looking awkward and out of place, now that she didn't have Madison and me to herself. My present from my best friend had been a bust. And we were having *dumplings*.

Mrs. Jameson cleared off the kitchen table. Mom and Yi Po laid out the supplies—garlic, ginger, sesame oil, soy sauce, cider vinegar, Chinese chives, ground pork, and dumpling wrappers. Packages and packages of dumpling wrappers.

More girls arrived, and someone started playing music. I stood in the doorway to the kitchen, hoping to block their view.

Yi Po looked like a TV chef on fast-forward. She swiftly mixed together the pork with the seasonings. Mom cut open the first package of dumpling wrappers and set out a small bowl of water on the table. Mrs. Jameson began filling up pots of water and setting them on the stove.

I looked at the clock. It was already 5:15. *By the time they're done, we'll have to rush to go trick-or-treating,* I thought. *We should have ordered pizza.*

"What's going on?" Serena poked her head in. "What's for dinner?"

"We're supposed to have dumplings, but there's been a small prob . . ." Before I could finish, Serena pushed her way past me into the kitchen.

"You guys are making dumplings? Wow!" she exclaimed. She picked up a dumpling wrapper. "Can I make one?"

Yi Po stopped and showed her what to do. She laid the wrapper in the palm of Serena's hand and added a dollop of pork filling in it. Then she dabbed her finger in the water and wet the half of the outer edge, and then closed the wrapper with a row of little pleats.

Yi Po held it out in her palm. *One perfect dumpling,* I thought, *and only about three hundred to go. And what's Serena going to say? Is anyone else going to come in?*

Before I knew it, more girls crowded by the kitchen door. They stared at Yi Po.

"Hey, you guys, you don't have to come in here. It's just dumplings, and we're going to order pizza," I said. I wanted to kick myself. Having dumplings was the worst idea in the history of birthday parties.

But Serena had a different idea. "Hey! Get in here! This is so *cool*!"

Did she say *cool*?

Haley went into class-president mode, all manners and meet-and-greet. "Hi, Mrs. Wu," she said to my mom. "Lucy, I know your mom, but I've never met your . . ."

"Oh!" I fumbled for a second. "This is my grandmother's sister, my great-aunt. Yi Po." I tensed for a second, waiting.

Haley and Yi Po each raised a hand and said hi. Even when Yi Po says hi, it sounds Chinese to me. Then Haley said, "How do you do that? How can you do that so fast?"

"That's amazing!" said Lauren. "I want to do that."

Talent slid into the kitchen. "I can help," she said. "I've done this before."

Mom, Yi Po, and Talent each helped one girl with her dumpling. Before I knew it, there were a dozen dumplings, the slightly misshapen ones joining the trim, pleated ones.

Madison brought in a few more chairs to crowd around the table. "I think the party's in here!" she said cheerfully. More dumplings began to fill the tray in the middle of the table.

I took a seat and looked around. Bethany and Kelly were cracking up at Lauren's dumpling, which looked more like a turtle. Haley and Madison got into a serious discussion about whether you should hold the dumpling in your right or left hand. Talent reminded everyone not to get meat on the edge, or the grease would make it hard to seal the wrapper. Everyone was having a great time.

"She's the queen," said Serena, nodding at Yi Po. "She's the Queen of the Dumplings." I double-checked her words to make sure Serena wasn't making fun of Yi Po, but she really seemed to mean it. And judging from the heads nodding around the table, everyone seemed to agree. Mom and Talent were good, but Yi Po seemed to have some extra trick for making quick, neat folds — she made two in the time most people barely made one.

Mom leaned over and translated for Yi Po. Yi Po laughed and said something in reply. I leaned forward to see if I could catch any words that I knew.

Mom said, "Lucy's aunt says that she's actually quite slow. There are many people who are faster than she is, and her arthritis has slowed her down quite a bit, too."

"No way!" exclaimed Serena. "That's impossible!"

Yi Po looked up and grinned at Serena while still making the dumplings, and at that moment, I realized the party wasn't going to be a disaster. Maybe it'd even be good or great. With everyone helping, we were actually going to make all the dumplings in no time. Maybe that's how dumplings were supposed to be made — everyone sitting around, making them together, while laughing and talking.

Then came the actual eating of the dumplings. I think all that work just made everyone hungrier, and even Talent said they were the best dumplings she had ever had. Mom and Yi Po set out little bowls of soy sauce, vinegar, and hot sauce so everyone could try different kinds of sauces. We ate so much that when we went trick-or-treating everyone groaned and complained about how full they were. I swear even my French fry costume felt tight.

"I am not eating *any* candy tonight," moaned Haley. "I will absolutely explode if I eat one more thing."

Madison took one bite of a Three Musketeers, her favorite, and then threw the rest back in her bag. "We're going to be *waddling* to Barcroft Oaks," she joked.

At the end of the night, Madison and I agreed that it was the best party we had ever had—so far. And the funniest part was, without a doubt, it wouldn't have happened without Yi Po.

Which made what happened the next day that much worse.

AFTER WE HAD AN ENORMOUS BRUNCH WITH SCRAMbled eggs and French toast, Mrs. Jameson gave me a ride home. I was looking through my Halloween loot— we had gotten full-size candy bars in Barcroft

Oaks—when I heard her say, "Oh, dear. What on earth happened here?"

I looked up and my stomach jumped. The tree in my front yard had been TP'd. The entire tree was completely covered in toilet paper, so thick in some places you couldn't tell there was a tree underneath. When the wind blew, the loops of toilet paper swayed in unison.

Dad and Kenny were already outside, cleaning up. Kenny was holding a trash bag open and Dad was pulling down the toilet paper with a rake. Our neighbor, Mr. Ellicott, was also outside, talking to Dad.

"It's such a waste," I heard him say to Dad when I got out of the car. "There must be twenty rolls of toilet paper up there."

"At least," agreed Dad, pulling down another rake full of toilet paper. "And this is after my aunt scared them off. Who knows what else they would have done?"

"Ah, well, Halloween tradition, I guess," said Mr. Ellicott.

That's it, I thought. *It's just some stupid random Halloween prank.*

"Hey, Lucy," said Dad when he saw me. "Put your stuff in the house and then come outside and help clean up."

I thanked Mrs. Jameson for driving me home, and got out of the car. And then I saw what else had been done.

My basketball hoop was destroyed. Sodden toilet paper balls had been smacked onto the backboard, making it look like it had a weird case of chicken pox. And the hoop had been pulled on until it was a sad mouth hanging down from the backboard.

"Hurry up, Lucy!" called Dad. "This is going to take all morning."

I swallowed hard, trying to ignore the sick feeling rising up from my stomach. *It has to be Sloane. She knows where I live.* The sentence started playing itself over and over in my head, changing the emphasis from word to word. *She* knows where I live. She *knows* where I live. She knows *where* I live. It was as if this terrible fact would change if I could just find a different way to say the sentence. But it only seemed worse each time.

Through the window, I saw Yi Po come into the living room. As soon as she saw me, she stopped and stared at me, and then turned her head slightly to look at the hoop. I wondered what she had seen, if the people she had seen were boys or girls, my age or older. I wondered if she had questions she wanted to ask me, the way I had questions for her.

When I walked into the house to drop off my bags and presents, Yi Po pointed to the front yard and said something. Then she raised the pitch of her voice and began talking more quickly, making it harder for me to understand. She raised one hand over her head, and then lowered her hand. The words flew over my head.

Mom walked in and looked at Yi Po. Then she said, "Yi Po says that she saw three girls last night, one very tall one. She says that you might know the other girls."

Yi Po had seen Gabi and Ariana, of course. And *tall* was definitely the operative word when it came to Sloane.

I tried to keep my face expressionless, but inside, I felt a *crack*. The carefully constructed wall I had kept between Sloane and the rest of my life was turning to glass, and Yi Po was holding a hammer.

"No," I said firmly. I shook my head. "I have no idea who would do this." I definitely did not want my parents to get involved. If they found out, they would make a huge deal over it, and in the end, Sloane would just have twice as many reasons to make my life miserable.

"Lucy, if you know who did this, your father and I want to know. This is vandalism," said Mom. "They have damaged our property."

I looked at Yi Po. She looked puzzled. I could almost hear her thoughts. *You know who these people are. Why aren't you saying anything?*

"Would you please tell Yi Po . . ." I hesitated— I almost said *I don't know who she's talking about*, but I changed it slightly ". . . none of my friends would do this." That was true, but really, the more accurate statement would be: *My not-friends did this.*

Mom translated for me. When she was finished, Yi Po turned to me, her eyes narrowed slightly. Not angry, but firm. Resolved.

"*Zhi dao le,*" she said.

I already know.

CHAPTER TWENTY-TWO

SIXTEEN DAYS AFTER HALLOWEEN CAME MY REAL birthday—I was officially twelve. Kenny woke me up by sticking one of his buds in my ear and blaring the "Happy Birthday" song from his iPod—the Beatles version. Then he bounced up and down on the side of my bed, singing in a high-pitched voice and cranking out a solo on his air guitar.

"Go away," I said from under my pillow, ripping out the earbud. "It's going to be your *death*day if you don't leave me alone." I shoved him off the bed.

Mom made cupcakes for me to take to school. I was a little embarrassed—twelve is kind of old to be taking cupcakes to school. On the other hand, everyone seemed to like them, including Harrison. Especially Harrison.

"Great cupcakes," he said, licking the last bit of frosting off his fingers. "Lemon is my favorite."

"Really?" I think Mom had made lemon because that

was the only box of cake mix in the house. I mentally filed away that little piece of information, under Cool Stuff About Harrison.

When I got home, Yi Po was in the kitchen, where it looked like she had been working for hours. The counters were full of prepped and chopped vegetables and meats.

I had been avoiding Yi Po as much as I could since the toilet paper incident. I felt like I had disappointed her, and I worried that she would figure out a way to tell my parents what I knew. What she thought I knew, anyway.

I tried to spend even more time on practicing my shots. Even though Dad had done his best to fix up the old hoop, every time I looked at the dinged-up backboard and lopsided hoop I felt like Sloane was laughing at me, mocking me. I had caught Yi Po giving me a few confused looks after I came inside after only a few minutes at the hoop, but I pretended not to notice.

Now she was doing something nice for me, which made me feel worse.

I had one ace in the hole. We'd been going to Mamma Lucia's for my birthday ever since I was three. The waiters there put a candle in my dessert and sing "Happy Birthday" in Italian. Maybe there was a way to get out of this dinner.

When Dad came home from work, I met him as he came in the door.

Dad drew in a deep sniff. "Something smells a-ma-zing!" he sang out.

Darn! I should have put a fan by the door to keep away the smells coming from the kitchen. "We're going to Mamma Lucia's tonight, right? Because we always go on my birthday?"

Dad ran his hand through his hair. "I leave all that planning to your mother, honey," he said. "Whatever happens, I'm sure we can work something out."

When Mom came home, though, things went downhill in a hurry. She and Dad had one of those whispered parental conversations with lots of hand gesturing and glancing at me.

When they were done, Mom came to me. "Honey, I know that sometimes we go to Mamma Lucia's for your birthday . . ."

"We *always* go to Mamma Lucia's for my birthday," I corrected.

"But," Mom cleared her throat. "But . . . Yi Po has been in the kitchen working on a special dish for you." She looked at me. *Tell me something I don't know.*

"Maybe we could have it for dinner tomorrow?" I said hopefully. *And maybe I'll get invited to Madison's house tomorrow.*

"Lucy, we'll go to Mamma Lucia's tomorrow. How can we go out when Yi Po has worked so hard?" said Mom.

Of course she was right. I had known that all along. "What did she make?" I asked.

"Noodles. She made *the* noodles for you, Lucy. Just like the noodles she made for Daddy in China. It's traditional to eat long noodles on your birthday, to symbolize long life."

Long life. Ha. With Sloane on my case, that didn't seem likely.

KENNY WAS SO EXCITED ABOUT DINNER YOU WOULD have thought it was *his* birthday. He kept pacing around the dining room table and rubbing his hands together while Yi Po finished up in the kitchen.

I, on the other hand, sat in my chair, arms crossed, stomach tight and closed. I consoled myself with one thought: *Maybe it won't taste good.*

Mom, Dad, and Yi Po marched into the dining room—a three-person parade. Dad was holding the soup tureen, Mom was carrying a cake with a candle in it, and Yi Po was waving a ladle. They all sang "Happy Birthday," except that Yi Po didn't know about the third line when the rhythm changes and you add the name of the person. She just sang "Happy Birthday to you" over and over.

Okay, it was kind of cute.

Yi Po put the ladle down on the table and went back into the kitchen. Then she came back cradling a brand-new backboard and hoop in her arms, struggling a bit through the doorway. She hefted it into my lap. For a moment I didn't do anything. I couldn't have been more surprised if Pat Summitt herself had delivered it.

I ran my hands over the smooth board and stuck my fingers through the white, nylon netting. It had been years since I'd had a good net on the rim.

All this time I had thought Yi Po was judging me, waiting for me to tell my parents the truth about what happened. But maybe I had been wrong.

I tried to think of something to say, but Dad went first.

"Yi Po insisted that we get you a new backboard. Mom and I weren't so sure, but Yi Po said that you needed it."

My heart rose, and in that moment, something became completely clear to me. Dad had meant, *You needed a new hoop to replace the old one*, but Yi Po understood that I needed to play ball, just as I needed to eat and sleep. And maybe she cared more about what happened to me than what happened to our house.

For the first time maybe ever, I looked at Yi Po, really looked at her, without being mad or annoyed or worried about how my Chinese sounded. Her eyes were shiny and a huge smile stretched across her face.

"Thank you," I said. *"Xie xie."* I hoped that she could tell from the tone of my voice that I didn't mean a *thanks* kind of thank-you; it was a thank-you-for-thinking-of-me-with-this-perfect-gift kind of thank you. And more than that, I meant thank you for believing in me.

I think she understood because even though she nodded and said, *"Bu yong xie,"* which means *no thanks necessary*, that huge smile never left her face.

Yi Po then busied herself serving the soup. I was served first, and right away, I could tell it was different. Broth from a can doesn't smell this good. It had the good chicken-salty smell, but also whiffs of ginger and scallion. It smelled *golden*.

She had to have made the broth from scratch. Just like my grandmother used to, when she simmered the chicken in a pot all day, slowly adding spices.

I dipped my chopsticks into the noodles, looped them around and took my first bite.

Mmmmmmm. I could see how these noodles were instantly recognizable to Dad—the way you know someone from their handwriting or the way they walk. They were just like Po Po's—so perfect you couldn't imagine them any other way. Fat slices of beef floated near the top, surrounded by sprigs of cilantro and rings of onion.

To my right, Kenny was sighing and chewing and swallowing and sighing.

And then I couldn't eat any more, not because I was done eating or because I didn't want to eat, but because a thousand thoughts and feelings began to rush through me. Because I had a new backboard and hoop. Because I had someone in my family who actually wanted me to play basketball. Because, in spite of not being at Mamma Lucia's, I was having a wonderful birthday. Because the noodles were so familiar and good, and because I suddenly remembered what my grandmother used to say when we told her how much we loved her noodles. She used to say, *They taste good because you can taste how much love I put into them.* And I could no longer deny that the person who made them loved me, and maybe, just maybe, I loved her back.

I jumped up from my chair and wrapped my arms around Yi Po. Mom has always said that Chinese are not as huggy and kissy as Americans, but her gentle hug felt as if she had been waiting for me all along.

CHAPTER
TWENTY-THREE

IT DIDN'T GET MAGICALLY EASIER FROM THERE. My Chinese didn't blossom overnight, though I did notice that I was understanding more and more. Yi Po picked up an English phrase here and there—she liked saying *high five*, and used it for everything, including when I took out the garbage. But things were definitely different and that was a good thing. Instead of a foggy glass shield between us, we now had a clear view of each other.

I even figured out the mystery of where she was going every day. One day I came home to sixteen old people sitting at card tables spread out over the living room and dining room. They were playing mah-jongg.

Yi Po waved at me as I came in and then introduced me with her arm around me. *This is my niece!* Everyone smiled and went back to their games, except for one man who immediately got up from his seat.

"Hi, Lucy," he said. His voice was light and careful, like footsteps on eggshells. "I am Mr. Chen. Your aunt has told us so much about you! I understand you are quite a basketball player."

"Thank you," I said, surprised. *Yi Po had been talking about my basketball?*

"I hope you don't mind us here," he went on. "The community center where we usually play had to close for some plumbing work. Your aunt said you wouldn't mind if we came here."

I looked over at Yi Po. She was looking at Mr. Chen. Did she have a crush on him? Did he have a crush on her?

I turned back to Mr. Chen, summoning up my best impression of a good Chinese hostess. "No, no, not at all," I said. "We're delighted you're here." I looked around the room. *What would Mom do? What would Po Po have done?* Then I got an idea. I went back to the kitchen and found some little bowls and put some Chinese treats in them—the ones that have about six layers of wrapping on them. I took the bowls back out and put one on each table.

Most of the players were too focused on their game to pay much attention to the snack. But some of the ladies

230

patted my arm and said *Thank you* or *You are so good!* I tried to act casual, like I hosted groups of mah-jongg-playing old people all the time, but on my way out of the room, I caught a glimpse of Yi Po. She seemed intent on arranging her tiles, but she was sitting up a little bit straighter and had an unusually pleased look on her face.

Maybe I wasn't ever going to be as perfect as Regina when it came to Chinese social events. But I figured I wasn't doing half-bad.

THE NEXT DAY WE HAD A SCRIMMAGE AGAINST A TEAM called the Avalanche. If Yi Po's mah-jongg party was all about politeness and hospitality, the scrimmage was about pain and hostility.

The main problem was the other team's point guard, a girl named Petra. Petra was one of those players that make me wonder if she's an older player sneaking on to a U-13 team. She looked about sixteen and made of brick. She probably outweighed me by fifty pounds.

When Petra came barreling down the court, it was hard to defend against her. I tried stealing the ball but she just blew by me. Coach Mike had a different idea. He wanted me to set my defense so that Petra would run into me and get a charge called on her.

What Coach Mike didn't seem to understand was that I felt like I was about to be hit by an eighteen-wheeler. When I ducked out of Petra's way at the last second, Coach Mike pulled me out of the game. "Look, Lucy, sometimes you're going to get knocked down. That's just going to happen. You've got to take it, okay?"

I nodded, even though I wasn't excited about the idea. And I was relieved when Petra hurt her ankle and sat out the rest of the game.

After the game, though, Madison had other ideas. She invited herself over to my house, and we sat upstairs, talking about it.

"I could have gotten really hurt," I said defensively. "That's all."

"Physical pain is no match for the pain of losing," said Madison. The Avalanche had beaten us by thirteen points. "Get up."

There was barely enough room for the two of us to turn around. Madison grabbed my desk and pulled it over to the wall. "Move the bookcase by your bed, and we'll have some room to practice," she said.

I had gotten so used to the wall I'd kind of forgotten that I *could* move it. Still, Madison had a point to make and it was too dark outside to play. I slid the bookcase over to the wall.

Madison tried to push a pile of magazines under my bed with her foot, only to find a collection of shoes. "Um, do you think maybe things are getting out of hand in here?" she asked.

I grabbed the magazines and dropped them by the stairs so I'd remember to put them in the recycling bin later. Then I put all my dirty clothes in the hamper, stacked up the books on my desk, and put my shoes away. Now we had room to play.

Madison had me stand at one end of the bedroom. "The trash can is the hoop, and you're defending. I'm coming and you're going to draw the charge."

Madison clutched a ball of crunched-up paper and came toward the basket. When I realized she was trying to come in from the right, I moved into position. *Wham!* Madison tried to take a shot but it flew wide to the left.

"Ow!" I yelled. I rubbed my backside. I had crashed into plenty of people before, but letting someone run into me on purpose seemed to hurt more.

"What's going on up here?" asked Mom. She was standing in the doorway with Yi Po. "It looks like a tornado has come through here."

"Oh, we were just practicing drawing a charge. You know, getting the foul called on the other person," said Madison cheerfully. "Lucy just did great!"

"Yay. Me." I groaned.

Yi Po motioned for us to run the play again. I got up — maybe Yi Po would see how tough it was to draw a foul. This time, Madison tried to use my desk chair to set a screen. I beat her to the spot in front of the basket and set my defense.

"Jameson goes in for the two," yelled Madison.

Bam! Madison slammed into me full force. The closet door shuddered as I crashed into it and then hit the floor. The paper ball went in.

I looked to Yi Po for sympathy.

"Zhan qi lai," she told me. She looked amused.

"What'd she just say?" asked Madison.

"She just told me to get up," I said, surprised by Yi Po's lack of sympathy. I got up on my feet, slowly. I felt like there should be a Lucy-shaped dent on the floor.

Yi Po pantomimed falling and then slapping the floor. She wanted us to run the play again and for me to slap the floor when I fell. Madison grinned and nodded before I had a chance to say anything.

Bam! Down I went. This time, though, I slapped the floor. The fall didn't feel so bad. I jumped back up.

Again, said Yi Po.

We ran the play four more times, and each time, I got better at taking the blow by slapping the floor. Yi Po didn't have to say *zhan qi lai* any more. I was getting up.

After Madison left, I grabbed the corner of the desk to put it back. Yi Po was in the bathroom, getting ready for bed, and I didn't want to hold her up. But as I looked around the room, I realized that even with all my stuff jammed against the walls, the room had begun to feel better. The space was like a deep breath, calming and energizing at the same time. It probably hadn't hurt that I'd put a few things away, either.

When Yi Po came to bed, she looked around the room approvingly. I had pushed my desk into one corner, and then put the bookshelf between the bed and the desk. The space between us was wide open now, except for a few dust bunnies on the floor.

In the early morning hours the next day, I could have sworn I heard the *fwap-fwap*s of someone darting down the middle of the room in slippers, a *wsssk* of paper ricocheting into the trash can, and a very small, satisfied laugh.

CHAPTER TWENTY-FOUR

Meanwhile, at school, it seemed that all everyone talked about was the basketball game, ten days away. *Are you going to play? Are you going to try out for captain? Who do you think will win?* None of the teachers would say who was going to be on their basketball team—I guess they were trying to psych us out. We all agreed that Mr. Bellock, the computer lab teacher, was definitely playing because he was the youngest teacher *and* one of the few male teachers in the whole school. We also agreed that Mrs. Jurgensen, one of the third-grade teachers, would *not* be playing because she was almost a hundred years old.

Every time I heard someone ask, *Are you trying out for captain?* I nearly jumped out of my seat. Between keeping an eye out for Sloane's tricks and figuring out what I would do if I actually became captain, it was hard to focus on what was going on in class. The common denominator between four-fifteenths and seven thirty-sixths?

The capital of Hungary? The main categories of scientific classification?

Who had time for this when I couldn't figure out whether it was better or worse to make captain? If I didn't make captain, the pressure would be off and Sloane would probably back off for the rest of the year. But I wouldn't be captain. If I did make captain, Sloane might just make things worse. Oh, yeah—and then there was the small matter of winning the game.

I was distracted by these thoughts on Saturday, at the last Chinese class before the game, too, until Jessie gave me a hard shove. "Pay attention," she hissed. "We have to act this out next week." She was still waiting to get her video phone.

Today's idiom was *There are no 300 taels of silver here*. It was actually a pretty funny one—it reminded me of those stupid criminal stories on the news sometimes. Jing Lao Shi explained that a tael was a Chinese ounce. This guy, Zhang the Third, stole 300 taels of silver. He was afraid someone else would steal from him, so he buried them in his garden. Then he put up a sign saying, *Nobody buried 300 taels of silver here.* Duh!

Zhang's neighbor saw what Zhang had done, so he dug up the silver and took it. But then *he* put up a sign saying, *And your neighbor didn't steal the silver buried here!* So to say there are no 300 taels of silver buried here means that a person who tries to hide something ends up giving himself away by protesting his innocence.

Jessie, who had appointed herself the leader of our group, assigned the parts. "You'll be the guy who buries the silver," she said, pointing to Adam. "You can be the thief who digs it up," she told Liane. "You make the signs, *in Chinese*, okay?" she told me.

"Um, okay," I said, squinting at the handout.

Jessie shook her head as if a fly was buzzing around it. "These idioms are so *weird*, you know? Like, when would you actually say any of these things?"

"I don't think they're that weird," I responded. "That one we did on the first day, *dong shi xi su*, eating in the east, sleeping in the west? That's kind of like saying, having your cake and eating it, too." *Is that me, defending the Chinese language?*

"Or the one about the old man who loses his horse?" Adam chimed in. "That's like, every cloud has a silver lining."

"Well, yeah," agreed Jessie, "except in the Chinese version, the silver lining might be made out of lead paint."

By the time Chinese school was over, my brain was practically overflowing. *Make the signs for next week. How many decent shooters are going to be on the basketball team? What if I make captain and we lose?*

I nearly walked right past Harrison. He was hanging out by the trophy case, where we usually talked for a few minutes, or as I called it, the best part of Chinese school.

"Lucy! Hey, Lucy!" Harrison was sticking his hand in my face before I realized what I was doing.

"What? Oh, Harrison. Hi!" I stopped walking and turned around. For a moment I forgot to be nervous around him.

"So is it true?" asked Harrison. "I heard you're going out for captain."

"Yeah, I guess," I said. Then suddenly I added, "Though I've been dealing with some folks who don't think short Chinese people should get too wrapped up in basketball."

Harrison laughed. "Like who?" Harrison was definitely not short. I guessed he was already as tall as Ms. Phelps.

I looked down, suddenly fascinated by the linoleum floor. That was stupid of me. Nothing good could possibly come from bringing up Sloane. "People," I said. For all I knew, Harrison liked her.

"I guess *people* have never heard of Willie 'Woo Woo' Wong, then," said Harrison.

"Who?"

Harrison grinned. "There's a park named after this guy in San Francisco, where I used to live. Willie 'Woo Woo' Wong. He was short and Chinese. He played at USF."

"You are *totally* making this up." But I knew he was telling the truth. I could tell.

"Look it up if you don't believe me. He was supposed to have a killer set shot."

We reached the top of the stairway and Harrison gave me one of *those* smiles, the one where his one dimple comes out. I felt like I was the only person in the world.

"You just forgot one little problem," teased Harrison.

"What?"

"The captain is going to be a boy. Not some girl!"

"Harrison!" I gave him a playful shove.

Big mistake.

"Boys . . . *huh*!" Harrison didn't get to finish his sentence. His foot slipped off the top of the step.

"Harrison!" I shrieked. I lunged forward and tried to grab his hand.

Harrison grabbed for the railing, but his backpack yanked him off balance. He half-stumbled, half-tripped down the short flight of stairs, his legs twisting in completely unnatural directions.

As quickly as it had started, Harrison was at the bottom of the stairs. I ran down the steps.

"Are you okay?" I asked, trying to keep my voice from getting too shrieky.

Harrison shook his head slowly. "Can you do me a favor? Can you go find my mom?"

MADISON CAME OVER THAT AFTERNOON SO WE COULD practice for the game. I told her the basics of what happened. Harrison's mom and Jing Lao Shi ended up having to help Harrison leave the building. He said he couldn't put any weight on his right ankle, so he limped out between the two of them.

I left out the part about the shove, and I tried not to sound like I was obsessing over it. Except I was. I had looked up his phone number in the school directory and had almost dialed it so many times that I'd memorized his number. I didn't tell her how I apologized a hundred times. Maybe he hated me.

I tried to concentrate on shooting. It was great having a net on the new hoop — the ball dropped down straight instead of bouncing wildly off the driveway. We played one-on-one and then did free throws. I got eight in a row.

"How do you do that?" asked Madison.

I shook my head. "I'm not sure. It's like I do better when I turn off my brain and let my body take over."

"That doesn't make any sense."

I tried to explain it. "It's like walking, right? You just do it now, you don't think about it. If you thought too hard about it—how do I bend my knees? where do I put my foot?—you'd probably trip a lot more than if you just did it."

"Whatever you're doing, just make sure you do it on Friday."

Friday was six days away. Did Sloane have any more tricks up her sleeve?

"Maybe Sloane will back off, now that she knows you won't quit," said Madison. It was as if she could read my mind.

"Uh-huh," I muttered. *Fat chance.*

"Let's do ten more," suggested Madison. "Then I've got to go."

But talking about Sloane had unsettled my brain. My arms shook and the ball flew awkwardly through the air and bounced off the top of the backboard. *Airrrrr balllll!*

I looked up Willie "Woo Woo" Wong that night. Harrison was telling the truth. Willie Woo Wong was five foot five and was called "the biggest little man in basketball." He was nicknamed "Woo Woo" because that's what the crowds used to yell when he played. Some people said that Willie Wong had a perfect set shot, and he once scored sixty-five points over three games during a tournament.

Way to go, Harrison, I thought. Then, *I hope you're okay.*

CHAPTER TWENTY-FIVE

SUNDAY STARTED OFF AS A QUIET DAY. NO BASKETBALL practice or Chinese school. No one fell down the stairs. Kenny went out with some friends. Mom and Yi Po had tea in the kitchen while I watched TV. Dad sat in the dining room and read the paper.

Suddenly, Dad came charging out of the dining room. "Do you know where Kenneth is?" he demanded. This was not good—Dad never says *Kenneth*.

"No," said Mom. "What's wrong, Steve? Has something happened?"

Dad pointed at the paper. On the front of the paper, there was a photograph of a group of high school students. The caption read *Roosevelt High School Mathwhiz Team Moves on to Regionals*. Kenny was nowhere in the picture.

"Maybe Kenny just missed the day they were taking pictures," I said hopefully.

"Maybe," said Dad grimly. Mom shook her head.

I closed my eyes and tried to send Kenny a telepathic message. *Kenny, stay away!*

KENNY DIDN'T GET MY MESSAGE—NO ONE EVER DOES. Right as Mom was bringing dinner to the table, Kenny came in. "Hey, guys, what's up? Sorry I'm late—lost track of time."

"You are in *trouble*," I said to Kenny under my breath. "There was a picture of the Mathwhiz team in the paper and *you* weren't in it."

"Oh, boy." Kenny's shoulders sagged, deflating. "I was afraid something like this might happen."

"So you . . ." I stopped when Mom came in and saw Kenny.

"Hi, Mom," Kenny said weakly. "Can I help with anything?"

"Everything's taken care of," said Mom, frowning. "Lucy, call your Dad and Yi Po."

When my parents get mad, they don't get mad in the same way. My mom gets very cold and unemotional, while my dad turns red and raises his voice.

Mom slid the newspaper across the table. "I'd like you to explain this, Kenneth."

Dad leaned over and stabbed the paper with his finger. "And you'd better have a very good explanation!"

They both stared at Kenny. Kenny stared at his plate.

"Did you miss the day of the photograph?" asked Mom.

Kenny shook his head. "I'm not on the Mathwhiz team anymore."

"But . . . but . . ." Dad scrabbled for the right words. "Your dream . . . Mathwhiz was your ticket to a good engineering school." My parents were always talking about Kenny becoming an engineer, like my mom, and what *amazing* school he would go to. They would recite the names like a Buddhist chant—*MIT, Caltech, Stanford, Harvey Mudd . . .*

Kenny's voice was small but clear. "It's not my dream—I'm not sure it ever was. I'll keep taking the upper-level classes at school, but I'm not doing Mathwhiz anymore."

"You have a gift," said Dad at the same time Mom said, "What will you do now?"

"I want," said Kenny, "to study history."

I could swear that I heard a *whoosh*ing sound in the room as both my parents inhaled at the same time. They had been fine with Regina being a Chinese Studies major, but she didn't have a gift for math like Kenny. In Chinese families, kids with math talents like Kenny don't become historians. They become doctors or engineers. It's practically a law.

"No," said Dad. "I'm not paying for you to go to college to study *history*."

Kenny didn't say anything, but I thought, *You can't force someone to become something they don't want to be, can you?*

AFTER MOM AND DAD'S FIGHT WITH KENNY, I WASN'T sure we were going to have a family get-together after dinner. We usually had one on Sundays. But as we were clearing the dishes, I saw Mom carrying The Big Green

Box into the living room, which meant we were definitely going to have one.

Some people use the word *scrapbook* as a verb. *I'm scrapbooking tonight!* For Mom, though, the word is just completely foreign. All our family photos, all our school pictures, any picture that someone might have sent us, went into what we called The Big Green Box, a large, dark green box that I think once held a pair of boots. Need a photo for a school project? Go get The Big Green Box. Want to know what you looked like five years ago? Look in The Big Green Box. While normal people sat around and looked in scrapbooks that might be organized chronologically, my family sat around The Box, pulled random photos out, and tried to figure out what they were and where they were from.

"We're looking through The Big Green Box tonight, huh?" I asked Mom.

Mom nodded. "I thought Yi Po might like to see some photos before she goes, and we can make copies of any pictures she would like."

This ought to be good. I could just see us plowing through haphazard piles of photos, looking for anything decent for Yi Po.

Me: This is Regina batting a piñata from her fourth birthday party!

Mom: Here's Kenny's second-grade soccer team that he quit halfway through!

Dad: This is Lucy when she was missing her two front teeth!

Yi Po (in Chinese): You guys ever heard of a *scrapbook*?

In reality, though, Yi Po didn't seem to mind looking at odd photographs of me riding a bike or even Christmas photos from neighbors who had moved away. She paid particular attention to pictures of Po Po, from birthday parties and the holidays. She smiled at each one and then set it aside so it wouldn't go back into the mysterious depths of The Big Green Box.

Kenny pulled out one and started laughing hysterically. We all leaned over to see what he had found.

Dad tried to yank it out of his hand but Kenny held it away.

It was a picture of a college student, wearing sandals, jeans, and a fringe jacket. He had on sunglasses and was carrying a guitar. His long black hair was pulled back into a ponytail.

I realized it was Dad. And he was *smoking*!

"Dad . . . is that . . . you?" I asked. Kenny was laughing so hard he could hardly breathe. "You . . . look . . . like . . . a . . . Chinese . . . John . . . Lennon."

Dad straightened his neck, trying to look dignified. "I guess some photos from your grandmother's house got mixed up in here," he said stiffly. "It was a brief stage I went through in college."

Dad plunged his hand into The Big Green Box and yanked out another photo. "Look what I found," he said with a note of forced enthusiasm in his voice. "A really old one."

We all turned to look at the small black-and-white photo. A woman and a young girl stood on the deck of a ship with the Statue of Liberty in the background. They were both squinting at the camera.

I stared at the photograph. I had seen the picture before, and just assumed it was from a family we didn't know.

"Look at those clothes," murmured Mom. "They don't dress like that anymore." The woman was wearing a dress, white gloves, and a hat. The little girl was also wearing white gloves and carrying a little purse.

"That girl looks a little like you, Lucy," said Kenny, "when you were her age." I looked harder but I couldn't see a resemblance.

Yi Po reached down and gently plucked the photo from Dad's hand.

I thought I'd never see this picture again, she breathed. For a second, she sounded so calm that I thought I'd misunderstood. But my parents and Kenny looked just as startled as I felt.

SLOWLY, SLOWLY, YI PO TOLD US THE STORY OF THE photograph. My parents translated. And Kenny explained until I had a whole story in my head, pumping through my veins and swirling in my heart. Until her story became my story, too.

It was the year after the Cultural Revolution began, when Chairman Mao began the Four Olds campaign. I was a young woman then. We were told, "Get rid of your Four Olds—old culture, old habits, old customs, and old ideas—bring China into the future!" Bands of Red Guards roamed the streets, entering homes to look for evidence of Four Olds. After a while, we started to recognize the sound of their terrorizing. The banging, the smashing, the screaming. Many times, people were dragged out of their homes for a "struggle session," where neighbors would be forced to watch the Red Guards beat, torture, and humiliate their victims.

One day we saw our neighbor, Old Zhou, lying on the ground. He had been kicked and pummeled by the Red Guards. We later found out he had been punished for trying to hide a single postage stamp from the United States. It was forbidden because it showed that he admired Western objects. He almost died from his injuries.

Then my aunt heard that we might be next, perhaps because my family had once been landowners. It was hard to know—anyone who once had money or who had an education was under suspicion. We looked quickly through our belongings, examining each one for any quality that might make it a Four Old. I did not think we would have anything that would displease the Red Guards—we just did not have much. But then, my aunt seized upon our photo album.

"Hurry! Look!" I remember her hands shaking as she leafed through the album. We tore out photos of older relatives, anyone who was in fancy or Western dress. I felt as though we were suffering their deaths once more as we ripped out their pictures—we would never see their faces again.

She turned the page. There was the photograph, a duplicate of the photograph you have here. It was the only photograph I had of my mother and my sister. How many times had I looked longingly at that picture?

"This one, too," said Auntie firmly, and she grabbed a corner and started to pull.

"Please, no," I begged. I grabbed her arm.

She shook her head. "We must." She continued to rip out the photograph.

I felt as if my heart were being torn out with the picture. "It's my only photograph of my mother and sister. Please. I'll hide it. I know I can hide it where they'll never find it." Of course I didn't know where I would hide it, but I had to try.

My aunt turned and glared at me. "You ingrate!" she hissed. "All these years I've cared for you as one of my own. Where were your mother and sister when you needed them? And now you want to risk this . . . this paper family for your real family. How dare you!"

In that split second, I thought I saw something else in her eyes. Not fear. A look of calculation, perhaps. Jealousy? Not for the first time, I wondered if she was jealous of the love I still had for my parents and my sister. Not for the first time, I wondered if she knew what had happened to them.

But then I hung my head. How could I be so ungrateful?

"Remember Old Zhou!" she cried shrilly.

I held out my hand. "Give it to me. You are right. Please, just let me take care of them."

The Red Guards often searched through the rubbish bins, so we couldn't simply throw away the photographs. We had to burn them. I shut the bathroom door and burned the photographs one by one. I saved that photograph for last.

I held the picture and stared at it, trying to memorize every last detail. The look in their eyes, the patterns on their dresses, their hair. Then I held it to my chest. "Forgive me," I whispered. Then I watched the photo curl and burn until there was nothing left but black ash.

The Red Guards did come. I found out later that a friend of mine had accused us of being counterrevolutionary to protect her own family, and that was what had provoked the attack. It was such a terrible time—truth, loyalty, honor meant nothing. The whole order of our society had been turned upside down.

I watched them ransack my home, tearing apart the beds, tossing drawers on the floor, and going through trunks. They seemed to delight in throwing our belongings around, stepping on them carelessly. I don't think I could have hidden that photograph, they were so thorough. But I did not flinch, I did not cry. They could not hurt me anymore.

· · ·

WHEN SHE FINISHED TELLING HER STORY, WE WERE ALL quiet for a moment. Kenny looked at my parents for a long time.

For the longest time, China had seemed like a separate place, the hyphenated place in my life. Chinese-American. But now China was close, because that's where Yi Po was from.

She had lost so much—her family, her history, even her friends. How did she ever manage to smile or feel happy again? I thought about the way she looked when she brought me the basketball hoop and backboard. Could I go through something so awful, and then care about making another person happy?

Zhan qi lai. Get up. You had to get up again.

I leaned against her, trying to give her the support my words could not provide. I wondered what my grandmother would have thought. I think she would have been proud to have Yi Po as her sister. If she could be that brave, maybe I could, too.

CHAPTER TWENTY-SIX

WHEN I WENT TO SCHOOL ON MONDAY, THE FIRST thing I did was look for Harrison. His desk was empty. I tried to get ready for the social studies quiz, but I couldn't help checking every few minutes.

Then, a few minutes after the bell rang, Harrison came hobbling in. He was on crutches. "Still getting used to these things," he said to Ms. Phelps.

I waited for Harrison to look my way, hoping for a smile or *something*. He didn't. *He probably hates me.* A heavy feeling of disappointment wrapped around me. *It was the best conversation we ever had, and look what happened!*

Finally it was time for lunch. At least I had lunch to look forward to. Instead of the usual peanut butter and jelly, I had lemon chicken—one of Yi Po's best dishes. I watched the clock tick toward lunchtime. I swear that the hands got slower as it grew closer to 11:20.

I grabbed my lunch and headed toward the cafeteria with the rest of my class. My mouth quavered in anticipation of the tangy lemon flavor blending with the gently steamed chicken. I eagerly unscrewed the top of the container.

Whoa. I dropped the lid and stared inside. There, on the topmost piece of chicken, was a small, dead cricket. It might as well have had a little card attached saying *Compliments of Sloane Connors.*

How did she do that? My mind raced back over the morning schedule. Social studies quiz, language arts, music . . . *ah, that's it.* She must have slipped into the classroom while we were in music class. It would have been easy for someone like Sloane, who was always running errands for the teacher. Haley and Serena were missing lunch right now because they were helping the art teacher, Mrs. Felsworth.

"Is that what I think it is?" asked Madison in a low voice.

"Yeah, I guess my good friend Sloane thinks I'm not getting enough protein."

"Throw it away," urged Talent. "We'll share our lunches with you."

I looked at the cricket again. Having once had a frog on my plate, I wasn't *that* grossed out by the cricket.

"I have a better idea. Is Sloane watching?"

Madison turned her head ever so slightly and checked. "Oh, yeah, you've got the whole Amazon crew looking."

I carefully dug my fork in, stabbing a piece of chicken away from the cricket. I lifted it up and ate with great relish.

"I don't know what's different, but this is the best lemon chicken *ever*," I announced. Shrieks erupted from the next table.

Then I waited. We had recess right after lunch, along with Sloane's class. For the first time in months, I didn't avoid Sloane.

I didn't have long to wait. Sloane, Gabi, and Ariana slithered over to me. I could have sworn that Sloane was panting with glee. Madison scooted over next to me until her arm was touching mine. Talent stood next to me on the other side.

"Hi, Sloane!" I said brightly.

Sloane looked a little surprised, and glanced at Gabi and Ariana. "Hi, Lucy," she said uncertainly. Then, gaining a little steam, she added, "How was your lunch today?"

"It was great. I had lemon chicken — one of my favorite dishes. And today it was even better than usual."

"Really?" Sloane turned and gave the Amazons a *look*. "Why do you think?"

I cocked my head to one side, pretending to think very hard. "Extra lemons?"

Sloane looked like she might explode. Then she burst out, "You ate a cricket! Oh, my God, you ate a cricket!" Sloane started cackling gleefully. Gabi and Ariana actually took a step away from her.

This is what I had hoped for. "Don't be silly, Sloane," I said deliberately. "I know what a cricket looks like and I certainly didn't eat one. But I can't imagine why you thought there was a cricket in my lunch unless you put it there yourself." I raised my voice just a bit for the last sentence. *There are no 300 taels of silver here.*

Suddenly, Sloane realized what she had done. She stopped laughing just in time to see Ms. Phelps turn our way and tilt her head to one side. Sloane's eyes widened.

"Y-y-you don't know what you're talking about!" she stammered, and her group quickly scattered. A cool, pleasant feeling began to fill me up like a drink of water.

"That was awesome," said Talent.

I turned to Madison and Talent. "Wouldst thou like to play some basketball?" I said, using my best Queen of England accent.

Talent shook her head, holding up a book as an excuse. "Maybe next time."

But Madison said, "I couldn't imagine anything more delightful," in an equally haughty accent and we headed to the courts.

I WAS SO EXCITED WHEN I CAME HOME FROM SCHOOL that I ran around the house, looking for Yi Po. She was in the living room, reading a Chinese newspaper.

"*Wo zhe ge xing chi wu you yi ge lan cho bi sai . . .*"
Suddenly, I realized I was speaking Chinese without thinking about it first. *I'm having a basketball game at school this Friday . . .*

Yi Po put her newspaper down and listened.

Wait, did she have a mah-jongg game on Friday? *I know you have mah-jongg, but . . . will you come? And will you bring a can of food?* I finished. I was pretty sure that I had messed up about half the word order and maybe some of the pronunciation, but I had surprised myself. I did actually know all the words I wanted to use. I even remembered the word for *can: guan tou.*

Yi Po pretended to dribble a ball and shoot it. Then she cupped her hand into the shape of a can. Then she pointed at me.

I nodded.

A wide grin spread across her face. She held up her hand for a high five.

Maybe the best year ever was still possible.

CHAPTER TWENTY-SEVEN

I WISH I COULD SAY THAT THE REST OF MY FAMILY HAD an equally positive reaction when I invited them to the game that night at dinner.

Dad shook his head. "I've got a meeting Friday afternoon. We've already moved the meeting twice."

"I wish you had told me earlier, Lucy," said Mom. "I'll try to work something out but I can't make any promises, okay?"

I couldn't shake the feeling that if I had invited them to something like a science fair or even a spelling bee, they'd be trying harder to come.

"What about you, Kenny?" I asked. Kenny got out of school earlier because he was in high school, though he usually stayed for after-school clubs.

"An elementary school basketball game? I don't know . . ." He shoved a forkful of shredded pork and tofu into his mouth.

"C'mon," I begged. "They might have food." I wasn't sure of this, but it was the best bribe I could come up with.

Kenny took another bite of food and considered. "Maybe," he said.

ANY FEELINGS OF TRIUMPH I HAD ABOUT MY ENCOUN-ter with Sloane officially disappeared at 9:17 a.m. the next day. That's when Ms. Phelps made an announcement.

"The president of the PTA had a suggestion for this Friday's game. Instead of just bringing cans of food to the game as part of the food drive, you all will be using your cans to vote for a team captain," she said. "Each person will be allowed to vote with their can of food. So now the team captain will be determined by the number of free throws he or she makes, *plus* the number of cans of food he or she receives in the voting."

No way! My jaw nearly hit the desk. Now that Sloane knew she couldn't scare me off the court, she was getting *her mother* to rig things for her. I wanted to jump on top of my desk and yell *CHEATER!* The whole class began to talk.

Ms. Phelps pressed her lips together and frowned. It's the face she makes when she's trying not to yell at us.

"Obviously, this isn't what was planned in the beginning, but in any event, please be sure to bring your cans of food to school on Friday and vote for your pick. Now, moving on to today's test on fractions . . ."

I wasn't sure, but I thought Ms. Phelps seemed kind of annoyed by the whole thing, too.

"That's it, I'm sunk," I said at lunch. "There's no way I'll get to be captain now."

"I'll vote for you," said Madison. "And so will Haley, Serena, Lauren, and a bunch of the other kids. We'll bring lots." Haley and Serena nodded in agreement.

"Mrs. Connors knows tons of people through the PTA. She's here all the time, right? She'll get everyone to vote for Sloane." I slouched in my chair.

"You can't give up, though. Not now. You can't just

let her be captain without even taking a shot," argued Madison.

I thought of something else. "You know, all this time, we haven't been thinking of anyone else who could be trying out for captain. Other people will also be trying out, you know, to give Sloane some competition."

Madison narrowed her eyes at me. "Find me someone who can sink a free throw like you."

I knew that Madison was getting annoyed with me. But I was fed up. I had officially had Enough of Sloane Connors.

"We'll just see about that," I said.

DURING RECESS, I WENT OVER TO THE BASKETBALL GAME some of the boys had every day after lunch. I usually didn't play with them because they didn't play by the rules all the time. I swear I once saw Paul Terry take about a dozen steps without dribbling the ball on his way up to the basket. Hello? It's called *traveling*.

I stood watching them, waiting for a break in the action. Eventually Paul subbed out to take a break.

"Hey, Paul," I said in a low voice. I was a little nervous. I didn't talk to Paul much, and he was about ten feet taller than me.

"Hey," he said. He didn't even look at me. He was too busy watching the game.

"So . . ." I was beginning to wish I hadn't started this. "Are you . . . you're going out for captain on Friday, right?"

Paul made a *hork*ing sound in his throat and spit into the grass. *Ewww.* "Nah," he said. "I don't think so."

"Why not?" I was really surprised. Out of all the sixth grade boys, Paul seemed a surefire bet.

"She . . . I mean *I* . . . I figure I'm so much taller than the rest of you guys, you probably wouldn't be able to play my style. So . . . no."

Wait a minute . . . *she*? "Is this what you think, or is this what someone told you?" I asked.

"Does it matter?"

"Sure it does," I said. *Sloane had gotten to him.* "But you're playing, right?"

"I dunno," Paul muttered. "It's just some dopey school game, anyway."

"Look, we need you," I said. "We need some big guys on the team or we won't have an inside game against the teachers."

Paul half-smiled. I think he liked being referred to as a *big guy*. "You're taking this awfully seriously," he said.

"Just say you'll play."

"Yeah—I might."

"Great," I said. I hurried away, looking for other kids.

Oscar, who has great speed and good ball-handling skills, said he wasn't trying out for captain because "his English not so good." I heard that Jeremy, a kid in Mrs. Tibbs's class with a nice outside jumper, was holding back because Sloane said she *might* go to the dance with him if we had one. Teresa, who had played basketball with Madison and me last year, just shook her head and folded her lips shut when I asked her about it.

Sloane. Sloane had gotten to them all except me.

I made them all promise to play. And I asked them all to vote for me.

CHAPTER TWENTY-EIGHT

THE DAY HAD FINALLY COME. WE WERE ALL STANDING in the gym, the sixth-grade basketball team. The whole school was watching us.

In the crowd I could see Mom, Yi Po, and Kenny. And there was Regina. Regina! I couldn't believe she had made it. Dad wasn't there, though. But there was no time to worry. Everyone quieted down. Mrs. Nicholson, the principal, was speaking into the microphone. Her hair was braided into dozens of little braids and she was wearing a royal blue suit.

"Before the actual game begins, we have a very exciting contest between Sloane Connors and Lucy Wu to determine who will be captain of the sixth-grade team. As you all probably know, the captain will be determined by who has had the most people vote for her by way of bringing in cans of food, plus the number of free throws she makes.

"As it happens, Sloane and Lucy received the exact same number of cans, one hundred and twenty-seven! Therefore, it all comes down to the free throws. Without further ado, I would like Ms. Wu to step to the free-throw line."

A bolt of nervous energy shot through me. This was exactly what I had hoped for. Bring on the free throws!

I stood on the line, dribbling and studying the hoop. The edges of the backboard glowed from the bright lights, making it a little hard to see the basket.

Breathe in, breathe out. Don't overthink. Just shoot.

I released the ball, letting my hand drop as the ball spun away. Perfect form. I watched the ball race through the air, heading straight for the basket. *It's going to be nothing but net.*

At the last second, though, something odd happened. The ball just fell away from the hoop, as if a giant invisible hand had slapped it away.

For a moment, there was complete silence in the gym. Then I heard the tiniest giggle, which started in one corner and rippled outward. Everyone was laughing! Cackling, snorting, snickering filled the air. Mrs. Nicholson was laughing! I looked over at my family. My dad was there now, and my whole family had their heads thrown back, laughing so hard that I could see their back teeth. Even Madison looked like she was trying not to laugh.

I wanted to die. I wanted to slink out of the gym and start a new life, one that didn't involve basketball or mean families. A new life with a new best friend.

But I couldn't leave. A giant cricket was standing in the doorway, holding my lunch. Pat Summitt was standing next to the cricket, shaking her head.

I sat up in bed, trying to grasp the darkness around me. The only sound now in the room was my breathing. I looked at the clock. It was 2:07 a.m. In the other bed, Yi Po was fast asleep.

It was just a dream, I told myself. *Everything's going to be fine.* I tried to find a comfortable position and go back to sleep, but nothing seemed to work until a few minutes before I had to get up.

CHAPTER TWENTY-NINE

FRIDAY, THE DAY OF THE BIG GAME, HAD FINALLY arrived. I couldn't pay attention at all in class. I missed four words—four words!—on the weekly spelling test. My brain just wasn't there. Instead of *triumphant*, I wrote *trumpet*. I think I could spell only one word today.

Basketball.

After what seemed like several lifetimes, Ms. Phelps finally announced that any students wishing to participate in the basketball game should go to the gym to warm up. Madison and I stood up. Across the room, I saw Oscar stand up, too.

That was it? No one else was playing? While everyone had been *talking* about the game, not that many people actually planned on *playing* in it.

This was a problem. I had decided that since the teachers were taller than most of us, we needed lots of players to sub in and out to run them into the ground. We needed more players. The three of us looked around

274

the room, and the other students all stared back. Ms. Phelps looked a little worried.

"It's just for fun, guys. Even if you think you might want to play, you should go."

I saw Oscar nudge Andrew, and he stood up reluctantly.

"Hey, Haley, Serena, come on," I said between my teeth.

Serena shook her head. "I've got a gymnastics meet this weekend. My coach will kill me if I get hurt in a basketball game."

"Haley?" asked Madison.

Haley wrinkled her nose. "It's really not my thing. And you know, there are other players in Mrs. Tibbs's class."

I'd prefer teammates who are not out to get me, I thought. Then I heard a small voice say, "I'll play."

I turned around. It was Talent. Talent, who did not play basketball and who was the one person who kept me from being the shortest person in the class.

I swallowed my disappointment and tried to look

275

appreciative. She was willing to play, right? "Great, let's go," I said.

When we got to the gym, the teachers were already there, warming up. A couple of the teachers from the younger grades were there, along with Mr. Bellock, as we had guessed. There was also another tall lanky man who looked vaguely familiar.

"Do we know him?" I asked Madison.

Madison stared at him for a moment. "I think that's Ms. Phelps's boyfriend. Doesn't he look like the picture that Ms. Phelps has taped inside her closet?"

We watched him dribble up to the basket and put in an easy layup. This was definitely not fair. Who said boyfriends of teachers could play?

That wasn't the biggest surprise, though. *That* came when Mrs. Anderson, the librarian, trotted into the gym wearing a powder blue gym suit and matching glasses fastened with a head strap. Mr. Bellock tossed her the ball. We watched her square up for a three-pointer and fire one in.

Who knew?

Mrs. Jurgensen wasn't playing; she was assigned to watch over our team. She moved her head slowly from side to side, like a turtle.

"You all are the student team, are you?" she asked me.

"Yes, ma'am," I answered. I didn't usually say the word *ma'am*, but something about Mrs. Jurgensen made me use it.

She frowned. "I don't approve of these things. Students and teachers shouldn't play basketball together. Let's get this nonsense over with."

I turned to our group, which now also included Paul, Sloane, Ariana, Gabi, and Jeremy. "Okay, they've got ringers, but I think our best strategy is to keep them running. Anytime there's a breakaway, we should pass the ball up to Paul because . . ."

"Um, *excuse me?*" Sloane interrupted. "I don't believe anyone made *you* captain, Lucy."

"I'm not saying I am," I countered. "I'm just throwing out ideas."

"Hey," said Oscar. "Let's just do the shooting around. We have not much time."

Madison leaned over. "Sloane wouldn't know a good idea if it came up and bit her on the butt," she said in a low voice.

The other grades started to filter in, walking past the two large boxes marked *Sloane* and *Lucy*. I tried not to look. I could hear them whispering, trying to figure out who to vote for, and then a *clonk* as each can went into one of the boxes. *Clonk, whisper, clonk, clonk, whisper, clonk, clonk, clonk.*

I couldn't take it any longer. *If I'm way behind Sloane, I'll just die*, I thought. *Just look—it can't be any worse than not knowing.* I peeked just in time to see a little boy, maybe a first grader, carefully putting a can into the box marked *Lucy*. The boxes looked about equally full.

Okay, so far, so good. And my class was still coming.

But then a voice pierced the murmuring of the crowd.

"Sloooooooaaaaaaaannnnnnneeee!"

Mrs. Connors came marching into the gym, carrying a huge flat box of canned tuna fish. There must have been about thirty cans in it. They looked heavy.

"Slooooaaaaannnnneee!" crooned Mrs. Connors. "I brought those cans from Megamart, just like you asked. See?"

Sloane mouthed a sickly-sweet *thank-you* to her mom. I couldn't decide who I hated more at that moment, Sloane or her mother.

Then, Ms. Phelps walked in with the rest of my class. Most of the kids voted for me, though a couple stopped and studied the two boxes. I looked away when Harrison made his vote—I just didn't want to know. Ms. Phelps immediately went over to Mrs. Connors and pointed at the huge pack of tuna.

I was supposed to be warming up, but I couldn't help dribbling very softly so I might hear what was going on. I heard *not quite fair* and *but it's for charity*. Both Ms. Phelps and Mrs. Connors had tight smiles on their faces that didn't match the looks in their eyes. Finally Ms. Phelps walked away, hands on her hips, and Mrs. Connors cheerfully put the whole flat into Sloane's box.

This is not good, said half of my brain. *Just focus on the game!* commanded the other half. *You can make it up in free throws!*

I looked again. The boxes were definitely lopsided now, in Sloane's favor.

Mrs. Nicholson tapped the microphone. "I want to thank you all for coming to our first faculty–sixth grade basketball game and food drive. It's so exciting to see all this food for our local food pantry, and we're about to see a great game between our sixth grade and faculty."

She was actually wearing the royal blue suit that she had had on in my dream. This could not be a good sign.

Everyone began hooting and clapping. I jiggled my leg, trying to shake out my nerves. I scanned the crowd. I didn't see anyone from my family. Not even Yi Po.

Mrs. Nicholson started making a bunch of boring announcements. *Please hand in your gift-wrap orders this week. Parents, please save your box tops and soup labels to get more points for our school. Fifth-grade strings will be holding a concert next Thursday evening at seven.*

If it was possible to explode from stress, I would have been in little pieces all over the ceiling. *This is a terrible idea. Why am I here? I am going to make a fool of myself in front of the entire school.*

Finally, Mrs. Nicholson finished the regular announcements. She glanced over at the small group of mothers who were counting up the cans of food. "While we're waiting for a final count on the food donations, let's get started on those free throws," she declared.

I held my breath. Was it my turn?

"Representing Mrs. Tibbs's class, first we have Sloane Connors," she said.

I exhaled. I wasn't sure if going first or second was better, but suddenly I was glad I was going second.

Sloane stepped up to the line. She had on a pink tank top and matching shorts with double white stripes going up and down the sides. She also wore a ribbon in her ponytail in the exact same shade of pink. I glanced down. I had on a T-shirt from a summer basketball camp and my lucky pair of shorts that I had pulled out of the hamper.

"You can do it, Sloane!" yelled Mrs. Connors from the sidelines.

She dribbled three times and then brought the ball up to her face. She paused a moment, and she shot the ball, pushing both arms out straight. Her form wasn't great, but the ball seemed agreeable enough and went into the basket.

For the second shot, she dribbled twice and put more arc on the ball. It went in. For the third shot, she looked like she was shooting from one shoulder. That went in, too. I started to feel a little sick. Her form was terrible but her shots were going in.

On the fourth shot, though, Sloane started looking a little too confident and didn't even square up to the basket. The ball rattled around in the cylinder and then popped out.

"Ohhhhh . . ." said Gabi and Ariana in unison. A few more disappointed sighs rose up from the crowd.

Mrs. Nicholson picked up the basketball and expertly dribbled it a few times. Then she held it out to me.

"And now, from Ms. Phelps's class, Lucy Wu."

CHAPTER THIRTY

As I walked over to get the ball, I suddenly became conscious of the entire school watching me and every little thing about me. The way I swung my arms when I walked. The expression on my face. The tiny little squeaks from my sneakers.

Don't trip, I told myself. *Also, don't burp, fart, or look stupid.*

I took the ball from Mrs. Nicholson. She gave me a nice smile and whispered, "Good luck!"

"Go, Lucy!" shouted Madison. "Woo-hoo!"

A couple of people also clapped. That made me feel better. I looked around one more time for someone from my family—Kenny, my mom, Yi Po—but I couldn't see anyone.

Don't overthink it. It's you, the ball, and the basket. That's all you need to worry about.

I dribbled twice, bent my knees, and held my breath. Then I exhaled and released the ball. The ball floated through the air and neatly dropped into the net.

One. I had one. At the very least, it wasn't going to be a shutout.

"Keep it going, Lucy!" yelled Madison.

Keep going. Don't hurry, but don't stop for too long, either. Dribble twice, bend knees, hold breath. Exhale, release. The next two balls went in.

Now I was up to number four. If this one went in, I would beat Sloane in free throws. *Come on. You can do four in your sleep.*

The ball went up and caught on the rim. It rolled around the rim.

Please go in. Please go in.

The ball hesitated a moment and then slid through the net.

After that, I hit my groove. Five, six, seven. The crowd was starting to get excited. They started calling out the number after each basket.

"Eight." They chanted after the ball bumped the backboard and fell in.

"Nine." I could hear Madison slap the floor with her hands, the way we did during our games.

"Ten."

That's when I made my mistake. I looked into the crowd instead of keeping my eyes on the basket.

Harrison was looking straight at me, with the biggest smile on his face. He wasn't mad at me! He must have realized I was looking at him, because he picked up his crutch and gave a little wave.

Harrison isn't mad at me. He doesn't hate me! That's what I was thinking when I took shot number eleven, which might explain why the ball decided to fly out of my hands and hit the back of the iron and go out.

MAYBE THE ONLY THING WORSE THAN MISSING THE shot was having an entire gym full of people groan when I did it. I wanted to reach out, snatch back that moment in time, and do it over. And have my family there, too.

I thought of all the cans Mrs. Connors had brought in. The seven extra free throws I had made were not going to make up for that. I looked over at Madison. She was staring at the people counting the cans with a worried look on her face.

Mrs. Nicholson finished talking with one of the PTA moms and picked up her microphone. She motioned for Sloane and me to stand next to her.

"Let's give a hand for Lucy and Sloane, shall we?" She lightly clapped her free hand against the microphone. "They both did a wonderful job but we now have the results to determine the team captain for the sixth grade."

Mrs. Nicholson slipped on the glasses she wore around her neck on a little chain. Looking at a little piece of paper, she announced, "You should all be proud of yourselves. Together, we have collected four hundred and forty-nine cans of food for the Helping Hearts Food Pantry."

There was another burst of applause.

"So, without further ado, in an extremely tight contest, the team captain of the sixth grade team, with two hundred and thirty-four total points, iiiissss . . ." I closed my eyes.

That's all I heard, though, the *ssss* hanging in the air like a huge deflating tire. *S* for Sloane, it just had to be. But I didn't hear another word because there was a commotion like a flock of chickens at the door to the gym.

I OPENED MY EYES AND LOOKED. FOR A MOMENT, I thought I was in the middle of another dream.

Yi Po walked into the gym. Then Kenny. Then Mr. Chen. Then about a dozen other members from Yi Po's mah-jongg group. They were all carrying shiny red or blue cans that I recognized from the Chinese grocery store. They were also arguing in loud, cheerful voices in Chinese.

Kenny looked at me and lifted his hands, palms up. *Sorry*, he mouthed. *Got lost.*

"What's going on here?" snapped Mrs. Jurgensen. "I need time to give a math quiz today."

Talent jumped up and led Ms. Phelps over to the group. Ms. Phelps held out her arms to collect the cans as Mrs. Connors marched over.

What happened next was pretty funny, at least from where I was standing. Even from the back, Mrs. Connors was all furious angles and points. One elbow jutted out from her side. A long sharp finger slashed the air. It didn't help that she was wearing pointy shoes.

Meanwhile, Ms. Phelps was a cloud of round, soft happiness. Her arms curved protectively around the cans. A gentle smile lit up her face. She tilted her head to one side, listening to Mrs. Connors. Then I heard her say in a clear, sweet voice, "But if all of *your* cans counted because this is for charity, then certainly *these* cans should count also."

Go, Ms. Phelps! I cheered silently.

Mrs. Nicholson strode over to the two women and listened for a few moments. She must have been working some heavy principal mojo because when she was done talking, both Ms. Phelps and Mrs. Connors stopped arguing and looked very serious. She nodded curtly, and walked back to the microphone.

"Ladies and gentlemen, please excuse the slight interruption. I would like to say that the voting for team captain has *now* officially closed. And now it is time to announce the team captain of the sixth graders."

The entire gym held its breath. Mrs. Nicholson paused slightly.

"The team captain for the sixth graders is Lucy Wu."

CHAPTER THIRTY-ONE

I HAD ABOUT THIRTY SECONDS TO ENJOY THE MOMENT. Then I had a team to coach.

For the first half, my run-and-gun technique worked. I put myself, Madison, Oscar, Paul, and Jeremy on the court, and with five experienced players, we kept a slight edge on the teachers. My plan of feeding Paul the ball whenever there was a breakaway worked pretty well, until Ms. Phelps's boyfriend started guarding him.

I also discovered, though, that it's hard to play and coach the team at the same time. I barely had time to catch my breath and pull my thoughts together when I came off the court to tell other people what to do. I decided to stick to coaching for a while, which meant that after Andrew subbed in, the only fresh legs we had were Talent, Ariana, and Gabi. Not exactly the dream team. Sloane was nowhere to be found.

The lead slowly began to slip. Our four-point lead sank to a two-point lead. Then right before the break,

Mrs. Anderson drained a three to put the teachers up by one.

"Way to go, Barb!" shouted Mrs. Jurgensen as Mrs. Anderson sprinted by. I had to smother a laugh. Mrs. Jurgensen seemed to care about the game now that the teachers were ahead.

As my team came off the court at halftime, I handed each player a water bottle, urging them to drink and get a little rest. Paul drank half his bottle in one gulp. Oscar crinkled his bottle nervously. I wanted to think of something brilliant to say, but I couldn't. "Keep up the good work. We'll catch them soon," I said. But inside, a little voice said, *We're going to lose! And it's your fault.*

Several minutes into the second half we went down thirty-three to twenty-five, and the starters were looking pretty ragged. Mrs. Anderson's three-pointers were killing us. Madison was pressing her hand into her side, which I knew meant she was getting a stitch from running so much. And for all his showing off, Paul was clearly starting to fade during the breakaways. Oscar and

Jeremy were still hanging in there, but we needed more if we were going to win.

I checked my roster again, hoping a new player would magically appear. Nope. Talent, Sloane, Ariana, and Gabi. Talent was sitting at one end of the bench, but Ariana and Gabi traded whispers.

"Hey, Lucy," said Ariana in a low voice. "Lucy. Can you come here a minute?"

For a brief moment, I pretended not to hear her. I was entitled to a little payback, wasn't I? I turned and looked at Ariana with one disdainful eyebrow raised, the way Coach Mike looked at us when we missed an easy basket.

"Um . . ." stammered Ariana.

I waited. The tough coach act was kind of fun.

"Listen," said Ariana. "You have every right to be mad at us. It was just supposed to be kind of a joke, but it got out of hand." Gabi nodded.

"Anyway," said Ariana. "We feel like dorks just sitting here while Sloane is pouting in the bathroom. I just wanted to tell you that if you play us, we'll play for the team. No tricks, okay?"

I studied Ariana. I had no reason to trust her or Gabi, but then again, if they started messing around, I could yank them off the court and have the entire school as my witness. They had played once—they had that in their favor.

"You have two minutes to show me you're serious," I said. "Madison! Jeremy!" I called. "You are coming out."

Madison gave me a thunderstruck look when she saw Ariana and Gabi. I knew what she was thinking: *Are you crazy? Those two?*

Fweet! The game started back up and Oscar, Paul, Andrew, Gabi, and Ariana were in. The teachers had possession, but Gabi reached around and neatly stole the ball from Mr. Bellock. She passed the ball to Ariana, who drove past a second-grade teacher and flipped the ball in for two points. Madison nodded approvingly. Now it was thirty-three to twenty-seven.

Not bad. Gabi and Ariana still had some moves.

Mrs. Anderson hit another three. I made a mental note to Google her when I got home. Maybe she had gotten her library degree with a basketball scholarship.

Oscar threw a long, arcing pass down the court to Paul. Paul tried to showboat the ball in, and ended up missing.

I looked at the clock. Only four minutes left.

Paul and Andrew signaled for substitutions. I tapped Madison and Jeremy to let them know they should go back in. We were down by nine.

Ms. Phelps's boyfriend missed a shot, and Jeremy immediately got the rebound and passed it to Madison. Madison got into the lane and had to send up an off-balance attempt as Mr. Bellock lunged to block her. The ball went in on a prayer.

We were down by seven. Thirty-six to twenty-nine.

Madison made two critical plays. She stopped a fast break by the teachers and hit a three. And when Jeremy missed a pass, Madison dove for the ball and kept it alive as she slid out of bounds. Oscar picked it up for two points.

"Get back in there!" I screamed as Madison scrambled to her feet. "We can do it!"

Mrs. Jurgensen gave me a long look and snorted.

Now it was thirty-six to thirty-four. We had just under ninety seconds left. We were still behind, but I could feel the sweetness of the momentum swinging in our favor. I looked into the stands. Mom was sitting with Yi Po. She could see me win this game.

Behind me I heard a small polite cough. It was Talent. "The game's almost over," she said. "Aren't you going to play me?" She didn't sound mad or even like she was dying to get into the game. It was just a reasonable question. *Aren't you going to tie your shoe? Aren't you going to play me?*

As far as I knew, the last time Talent played basketball was during last spring's school carnival at the mini basketball booth. A sickening feeling washed over me.

You have to play Talent—she's your friend.

You can win if you don't play Talent.

I had wanted to be coach so badly, to show everyone that I could win. For just a second, though, I wished I could disappear. What would Pat Summitt do?

But then I did know. Pat Summitt might not play Talent. But I would. "Talent!" I made myself shout her name so I couldn't back out. "Can you shoot from the three?" I asked.

Talent's face lit up for a second and then faded. She shook her head.

"Can you take the ball on a fast break?" I asked.

Talent shook her head again, looking more confused.

I grabbed her by the shoulders and pointed her at Mrs. Anderson. "Great. You're perfect. I don't want anyone who's going to be a ball hog. I want someone who will stick to Mrs. Anderson like a Post-it note. *Do not let her get the ball. If she gets the ball, do not let her shoot.*" I put my hands up high. "Make yourself as big and annoying as possible, got it?"

Talent pulled herself up straight and nodded. "Got it."

The teachers called a time-out. Gabi and Ariana stepped off the court, breathing hard. "Good job, guys," I said, and I meant it. "I didn't know you could play like that."

"Huh," said Ariana. "Sloane did. But she said we shouldn't try out for captain because we weren't leaders."

"Yeah," added Gabi. "She said we couldn't think for ourselves."

I pictured Ariana and Gabi as two sheep, *baa-baa*ing in agreement to everything Sloane said. I felt kind of sorry for them.

The whistle blew, signaling the end of the time-out. I grabbed Talent's arm and together, we stepped onto the court. I wasn't going to miss the final seconds of this game, not for anything! I checked the scoreboard. Thirty-six to thirty-four. Sixty seconds left.

Ms. Phelps's boyfriend hit a jumper for two. Then Oscar hit a beautiful, nothing-but-net shot from the top of the key to give us three. We were down by one, thirty-eight to thirty-seven.

Now the teachers had possession with thirty *loooong* seconds on the clock. All they needed to do was to kill some time and then let Mrs. Anderson make one of her incredible threes to seal the game.

The entire gym was on its feet. The air shook.

I pointed at Mrs. Anderson, who was moving swiftly, trying to shake off Talent. Even though she was not the most naturally athletic person you'd ever meet, Talent was doing a really good job following the directions I had given her. She stuck to Mrs. Anderson like gum on the bottom of a shoe. "Watch her! They're going to give the ball to her!" I screamed at the rest of the team. Madison slid toward Mrs. Anderson.

But I was wrong. With no one covering her, Ms. Felsworth, the art teacher, took the ball and started to make a break down the court.

"Take it to the rim, Sandy!" screamed Mrs. Jurgensen. She was practically jumping out of her seat.

We've got to get the ball back. Out of the corner of my eye, I saw Talent sweep away from Mrs. Anderson. She ran to the middle of the court, and planted herself firmly in the path of Ms. Felsworth.

I think Ms. Felsworth was like me—she couldn't believe what she was seeing. Even though she had two or three steps to change course or pass the ball, she slammed straight into Talent. Talent flew backward.

Fweet! The ref stopped the game and ran to the middle of the court. Ms. Felsworth leaned down and helped Talent back to her feet. The gym became disturbingly quiet.

"Are you okay?" Ms. Felsworth asked.

Talent brushed herself off. "I'm okay," she said cheerfully. Then turning to the referee, she asked, "That was a charge, right?"

I shook my head, trying to absorb what had just happened. *Talent had drawn a foul!* She had made Ms. Felsworth commit a foul, and now we had possession of the ball.

I jogged over to Talent. "How did you know to do that?" I asked. "Draw a foul?"

Talent lifted her chin. "I read a book. You and Madison like basketball so much, I wanted to see what the fuss was about."

She read a book to understand basketball? Had she ever heard of a television set? I couldn't believe it—this was our chance to lock up the game because . . . Talent had *read a book on basketball.*

I called my last time-out. Eleven seconds left.

"Paul, you're going to inbound the ball. Just in case they decide to foul us, get it to someone who can make free throws."

"She means herself," said Madison, jerking her head at me. "Get it to Lucy, and the game's sealed tight."

Paul grinned. "Yeah, I saw what she did earlier."

"Just get the ball to the right person," I said, hoping that Paul would get my drift. I was pretty sure any of us could make the shot—except Talent.

We put our hands in and yelled, "ONE! TWO! THREE! LET'S GO!"

The ref handed Paul the ball and blew the whistle. We had five seconds to inbound the ball.

Five.

Mrs. Anderson planted herself in front of me. I tried to cut around her, but she stuck with me. Paul looked over at me, hesitating.

Four.

Paul checked his other options. The four other teachers were swarming around Madison and Oscar, choking us off from a decent inbounds shot.

Three.

I glanced over to the far side of the court. Talent was standing alone, completely unguarded. Like me, the teachers had figured she wouldn't pose a threat.

Two.

I pointed to Talent.

Paul: What?

Me: GIVE THE BALL TO TALENT!

One.

Talent was, perhaps, the most surprised of anyone in the gym that she was getting the ball. She nearly dropped it as the ball flew into her hands, but managed to hang on to it by trapping the ball between her forearms and stomach.

Now the clock started running. There were eleven seconds left.

The teachers turned and began racing toward Talent. At the same time, Talent realized that she had better change position, quickly.

Mrs. Anderson bore down on Talent with the swiftness of a well-oiled library cart. *DON'T PASS THE BALL YET,* I mentally commanded Talent. Mrs. Anderson could easily intercept a long pass from Talent. I wanted to get closer to Talent to get the ball and take the final shot.

For the first time in my life, one of my mental messages actually worked! Talent did not try to pass the ball. Instead . . .

Talent took a shot. *No! No! No! Why did I put her in?*

It was a midcourt heave that was so crazy-ugly that everyone just stopped to watch it tumble through the air.

Hit the backboard.

Bounce off the rim once, twice, three times.

And go in.

The shot went in.

A collective scream erupted. The crowd lifted up and rushed the court. Madison grabbed me. "We won! We won!" she screamed. Her whole face was bright and shiny with sweat.

"*You* did it. We did it," I said, and I meant it. I pointed at Talent, who was getting mobbed. "And there's the star who clinched the game."

Madison put her arm around me. "You know, only a truly great coach would have known to put her in."

"Maybe," I said.

Mrs. Jurgensen glared at me. I felt sorry for her class.

"Great game, Madison." Jeremy appeared next to Madison. Madison gulped and nodded. Even though her face was red from running up and down the court, she turned one shade redder.

I took off through the crowd. Only one person could make this moment sweeter for me — Yi Po. Yi Po and her perfect basketball gift and her mah-jongg club that I may or may not have invited with my imperfect, tone-deaf, wonderful Chinese.

When I found her, Yi Po was laughing, she was so happy. When she saw me, she held up one hand in the air.

"High five," she said.

I slapped her hand, and then grabbed it, pulling Yi Po with me through the crowd. It was time to make a few things clear. We walked together until I found the back of a certain person with a pink-ribboned ponytail.

I tapped her on the shoulder and waited for her to turn around.

"Sloane," I said. "This is my great-aunt, my Yi Po. She's my grandmother's sister, from China." I put my arm around Yi Po, just to make sure Sloane understood. Then I turned to my aunt. "This is Sloane."

Yi Po looked Sloane over carefully, and nodded slowly. Her meaning was clear: *I know you. I've seen you before.*

Sloane's eyes widened. *Halloween night.* Then she turned and walked away very, very quickly.

CHAPTER THIRTY-TWO

THE WEEKS AFTER THE GAME SPED BY.

Mom said I did a great job as coach and that I should definitely keep playing basketball to improve my leadership skills. Dad agreed. I wish it was enough that I love to play, but I'll take it.

For Thanksgiving, we had turkey, mashed potatoes, green beans, stuffing, cranberry sauce, corn, apple pie, and dumplings. Lots of dumplings. Regina came home for a few days and only complained about having to sleep on the living room couch a little bit.

Kenny started going out with this girl Lourdes in school who is on the Mathwhiz team, and he said he *might* go back to the team, but he's still going to study history.

After the game, Jeremy suddenly started showing up whenever Madison and I were playing basketball in her driveway. Madison acts all cool about it, but she misses a lot more of her shots when he's there.

Lauren said that Oscar said that Harrison said that he likes girls who play sports because they are more interesting and confident. *Hmmm!*

Sloane completely backed off. One day I even saw her eating lunch by herself, without Gabi or Ariana or any of the other Amazons.

Talent said she might sign up for basketball next year. *If* it doesn't interfere with Chinese school. She's already come over to practice a couple of times.

Regina came home from college for Christmas break with a buzz cut. When Mom saw that Regina had cut her hair shorter than Kenny's, she flipped out. Regina said that she was tired of being "objectified by her beauty according to the dominant male paradigm," whatever that means. She also got a lot of phone calls from someone named Derrick.

And Yi Po packed her bags and got ready to drive home with my Auntie Lin. She was going to visit with them for a while.

I sat on my bed and watched her pack. Her entire bed was covered with piles of clothes, shoes, toiletries, and books. Her slippers made their soft little *fwap-fwap* sounds as she shuffled back and forth, trying to figure out the best way to pack everything.

Once I hated all the weird little noises she made and the smell of her Vicks VapoRub, but they had become comforting ways of letting me know she was there. Now they would all be gone. It was funny—at first I thought that Yi Po was going to ruin my best year ever. Now I had a feeling I was going to miss her.

I didn't dare say anything. If I allowed even the tiniest crack, the entire dam would burst. I ran my hands over my quilt, feeling the little stitches and the cottony smoothness. The forsythia that Yi Po had sewn on my quilt was not so new looking anymore—it was starting to blend in with the rest of the quilt.

Maybe I should give her something to remember me by. Why hadn't I thought of this before, buying her a present? I looked around the room. I had a trophy from the student-faculty basketball game. I loved it, my first win as a coach, but it would be something for her to show her friends, to tell them about her time here.

I picked it up and walked over to her. At first she was too busy rearranging her clothes to notice me, but then she saw me, holding out my gift.

"Wo yao gei ni zhei ge . . ." I want to give you this . . . What was the word for *trophy*?

Yi Po took the trophy in both hands and looked at it tenderly. Then she gently put it back in my hands. *"Mei kong,"* she said simply. She had no space. But then she picked up the digital camera Dad had given her a few days ago. She put her arm around me and held the camera at arm's length. She wanted a picture of us.

"Deng yi xia," I said. *Wait a minute.* I took the camera from her and fiddled with the settings so that it could take a picture for us. I set it on my desk and flipped the monitor around so we could see ourselves.

We settled on my bed and stared at our tiny image. Yi Po gave me a little poke to make me smile. The camera whirred and clicked. I picked up the camera and examined the picture — not bad. We were both turned slightly toward each other, as if our picture were taken during a conversation. I showed it to Yi Po.

Then we both said, *"Ni xiang Po Po." You look like Po Po.* We both laughed. I closed my eyes and thought of five things about Po Po. She thought Hawaiian pizza was one of the greatest inventions of all time. She had one pair of jeans. Her favorite lipstick color was Blooming Rose. She remembered phone numbers in Chinese.

She had a sister. A sister who ruined my perfect year, and made it better.

I took the camera to the den so that I could download a copy of the photograph onto our computer. *Dian nao,* I thought. The Chinese word for computer literally means *electric brain.* I was still translating a lot of Chinese literally in my head like that, but my Chinese was getting better.

Mom came in and watched me set up the cable to the camera. She put one hand on my shoulder. "We're going to miss her, aren't we?"

I nodded, not trusting myself to say anything until I swallowed the lump in my throat. Mom squeezed my shoulder. "Yeah, we just took this picture," I said tightly.

"Good photo," she said.

I checked the settings to make sure that Yi Po still had a copy of the photo on her camera. Then I disconnected the cable.

"Mom, how do you say, *I will miss you*, in Chinese?"

Mom thought a moment. "You can say, *Wo hui xiang ni*."

I walked back to my room and handed the camera to Yi Po. She took it from me and tucked it into her carry-on bag. A bubble of laughter floated up from downstairs.

Just say it. You're going to be in a crowd of people soon, and you won't get to talk to her in private.

"*Wo hui xiang ni*," I choked out. As I said the words, I realized what they meant. *Xiang* was the Chinese word for *think*. *I will think of you*. I wondered if Yi Po knew that I meant more than that, that I didn't want her to go. Was I being too literal again?

I didn't have to wonder. Yi Po zipped up her suitcase and then turned and put her arms around me. Her eyes were bright.

"I will miss you, too," she said gently, careful to enunciate each word.

I will think of you. I will miss you. We understood each other perfectly.

ACKNOWLEDGMENTS

I would like to thank: the Society of Children's Book Writers and Illustrators and their Work-in-Progress grant program; my teacher, Mary Quattlebaum; my beta readers: Rebecca Borden, Carolyn Brady, Elizabeth Hadaway, Jennifer Buxton Haupt, Dorothea Starr LeBeau, Sharon Smith, Gretchen Starr-LeBeau; my fabulous Tuesday-night group: Anamaria Anderson, Moira Donohue, Marty Rhodes Figley, Anna Hebner, Carla Heymsfeld, Jacqueline Jules, Adele Leach, Suzy McIntire, Liz Macklin, Madelyn Rosenberg, Martha Taylor; Lindsay Davis and Ken Wright of Writers House; my editor, Lisa Sandell.

No acknowledgment would be complete without recognizing my sources of support: my mom, who told me I could do anything; my dad, who made me believe writing was in my blood; my husband, who wrote "writer" on our tax forms and has never (never!) once wavered in his support; our three beautiful, funny children; my amazing extended family; Fairfax County Public Library; A&J Restaurant, which makes absolutely inspirational bowls of soup. Get the Shanghai-style wonton soup.

ABOUT THE AUTHOR

Wendy Wan-Long Shang writes, "*The Great Wall of Lucy Wu* was inspired by a relative in China who was conducting genealogy research. When my mother sent him copies of family photos, he responded with awe and gratitude: He thought those images had been lost forever in the course of China's difficult history. In an age when a digital photo can be multiplied across the Internet in an instant, the idea of a lost photograph sent me searching for a way to connect a modern-day character to a very different time and place."

Throughout her life, Wendy has worked with children and books. She has been the office manager of a literacy organization, a juvenile justice attorney, a Court-Appointed Special Advocate, a tutor in elementary schools and a juvenile facility, and an early literacy volunteer with the public library. Of all the jobs, though, Wendy loves being a mother and author the best, always relishing the moment when a child finds that "perfect book" and can't wait to find out what happens next.

Wendy lives in suburban Washington, DC, and is the recipient of a Work-in-Progress Grant from the Society of Children's Book Writers and Illustrators. *The Great Wall of Lucy Wu* is her first children's book.